Talking
to Ourselves

Talking
to Ourselves

Andrés Neuman

Translated from the Spanish by Nick Caistor
and Lorenza Garcia

Pushkin Press

Pushkin Press
71–75 Shelton Street, London WC2H 9JQ

Original text © Andrés Neuman c/o
Guillermo Schavelzon & Asoc., Agencia Literaria
www.schavelzon.com

English translation © Nick Caistor and Lorenza Garcia 2014

Talking to Ourselves first published in Spain as *Hablar Solos* in 2012

This edition first published by Pushkin Press in 2014

ISBN 978 1 782270 55 3

Printed by CPI Group (UK) Ltd, Croydon CR0 4YY

www.pushkinpress.com

To my father, who is also a mother

Don't go thinking that what I'm telling you is something I tell everyone else.

—Hebe Uhart, "How Do I Get Back?"

Lito

Then I start to sing, and my mouth gets bigger. It makes Dad laugh to see how happy I am. But Mum doesn't laugh.

I'd been pestering them about it now for ages. Every summer. They always said the same thing. When you're older. I hate it when they say that. I picture a long line of kids with me at the end. This time they argued. Not out loud. They waved their arms about a lot. They shut themselves in the kitchen. It really annoys me when they do that. The kitchen belongs to all of us! I put my ear to the door. I couldn't hear much. After a while they came out again. Mum had a serious face. She looked out of the window. She blew her nose. Then she came over and kissed my fringe. Dad asked me to sit down with him. Like we were having a real talk. He squeezed my hands and said: You're a man now, Lito, we're going. And I started bouncing up and down on the sofa.

I try to stay calm. Well, I'm a man now, right? I pull down my T-shirt and sit properly. I ask Dad when we're leaving. Right now, he says. Right now! I can't believe it. I run up to my room. I open and close drawers. I drop my clothes on the floor. Mum helps me pack my backpack. This is going to be awesome. For sure. Totally. This is the kind of stuff that starts happening to you when you've turned ten.

All three of us go down to the garage. It always smells bad in here. I switch the lights on. And there's Uncle Juanjo's truck. Shiny. Like new. Dad starts checking the tyres. The engine. The oil. Does Dad know about things like that? Mum puts my backpack on the front seat. Right there. On the navigator's seat. I don't know what to say. We're silent until Dad's finished. His fingers are black. They look like insects. He washes his hands slowly. Then he climbs into the cab. He takes out his wallet and puts a photo of Mum on the mirror. She rubs her eyes.

It takes us ages to leave. We say goodbye and everything. Mum whispers in Dad's ear. She keeps hugging me. Oof. Finally we climb into the truck. Dad immediately straps me in. But he doesn't strap himself in. He examines some papers. Looks at a map. He writes stuff down. Suddenly the engine makes a noise. The door lifts up and the garage fills with light. I can't see Mum waving anymore. Well! Dad says, banging the steering wheel, let's hope Pedro brings us luck. Why is it called Pedro? I ask. Because it's a Peterbilt, son, he replies. What's that got to do with anything? I insist. Dad roars with laughter and puts his foot down on the accelerator. I hate people laughing at me when I ask questions.

I see the roofs of the cars go by. It's like being in a helicopter with wheels. One day I'll drive Pedro. Totally. I always watch the way Uncle Juanjo does it. There are hundreds of buttons everywhere. But they really only use three or four. The hardest thing has to be steering. What happens, for instance, if you're supposed to turn one way and you turn the other by mistake? All the rest looks easy because Dad doesn't seem to pay much attention to it. It's like he's thinking about something else. But I'm not going to tell Mum that. They always fight in the car. It'd be great to hold the wheel. But I know that's not possible when you're ten. I'm not stupid. We'd get a ticket.

It's super hot up here. I guess because we're so high up the sun is hotter. I try turning up the air-conditioning. I play with the buttons Dad played with when we were leaving. He pulls a face and turns it down again. I turn it up again. He turns it down again. Dad's really annoying. I ask him, just in case: Will you teach me how to drive? Dad smiles, then goes all serious. When you're older, he sighs. Just as I thought. It's illegal, isn't it? I say. That's not the reason, gun-toting mollusc, Dad replies. Why then? I ask, surprised. He keeps me guessing. Why? Why? I ask again. Dad takes a hand off the steering wheel, lifts his arm slowly (a red car passes us really fast, red cars are great, I prefer convertibles, a red convertible would be awesome, I wonder how the owners stop their hair from getting messed up, or maybe they all have it cut short?, of course, that must be it, but what about the women, then?), Dad stays like that, hand in the air, until I turn to look at him again. Then points his forefinger at me. No. Not at me. Lower down. He's pointing at my trainers. That's why, he says. I don't get it. It has to do with my trainers? Your legs, champ, Dad says, how do you think you're going to reach the pedals? Actually, I hadn't thought of that. What if I wore high heels like Mum? But I don't say that because I'm embarrassed.

We leave Pampatoro behind. The bar was really gross. The food was yummy. It had tons of ketchup. There are no more trees. The countryside is yellow. It's like the light is burning the ground. I read a sign: Tucumancha. There are loads of rocks along the sides of the highway. Orange-coloured rocks like bricks. Where do bricks come from? Do people make them? Or do they grow inside rocks and people cut them into squares? Pedro is very close to the edge of the highway. Dad is braking in a weird way. His back is very straight and he's gripping the steering wheel with both hands. It reminds me of *World Force Rally 3* (the music on the radio stops for the news, they read out: so many people dead, so many injured, the number of injured people is bigger than that of dead people, but what if some of the injured people die, do they change the numbers?, do they read them out again?, the music Dad has on is a bit boring, it's all old stuff), that video game has some great circuits, there's one full of rocks like a huge desert. Besides crossing it, you also have to dodge animals and shoot at Arabs who attack you. If you don't kill them quickly, they leap on your car, smash the windscreen, and stab you. It's awesome. Once I nearly beat the highest score. But I turned over at the final corner, lost a life, and got points deducted. Rally games are my speciality. Maybe it's because Uncle Juanjo has the truck. And without realizing it I've learnt too. Actually, now that I think of it, there aren't any pedals in *World 3*.

Dad, I say, did you know there's a game where the landscape is exactly like this? Really, he replies. It's one of my favourites, I tell him, the hardest thing is dodging the wild animals without driving off the track. Aha, Dad says, and if you drive off, what happens? You overturn, I tell him, and you lose time. What else? he says. Poor Dad doesn't know a thing about video games. And then you lose lots of places, I explain, and have to overtake them all again. Unless you find a supercharged engine or some extra-slick tyres of course. Is that all? Dad's being really annoying. What? I reply, you think it's easy dodging animals, killing Arabs, changing an engine, and overtaking everyone else without crashing into the rocks? No, no, he says, I'm asking what else happens when you have an accident, I mean, do you get hurt? Do people help you? Do you get to sit out a few races or what? Video games don't work like that Dad, I sigh. I give up. I'm not going to argue with someone who wouldn't even be able to beat the top score in *World 1*. I start fiddling with the radio until I find some better music. I look at Dad out of the corner of my eye. He doesn't say anything. We pass another sign: MÁGINA DEL CAMPO, 27 KM. There are no more rocks. The sun is almost level with Pedro. Now there are wire fences. Tractors. Cows. If we hit one, I'll have to restart the game.

Are you hungry? asks Dad. No, I reply. A bit, maybe. We'll stop again soon, Dad says looking at the map, that's enough for today. Then he stretches his arms (I don't think he should let go of the steering wheel, Mum always says that to him in the car, and Dad tells her he knows what he's doing, and Mum says if he knew what he was doing he wouldn't let go of the steering wheel, and Dad says she can drive next time, and Mum says he's unbearable when she drives, and they both go on like that for a while), he bends forward, twists his neck, sighs. His face looks tired. Hey, I say, why don't we eat some of what's in the back? No, Lito, no, Dad laughs, we have to deliver the goods intact. Besides, everything's packed into boxes. And counted. One by one? I ask. One by one, he says. And they count everything again after we've made the delivery? I ask. I really don't know, Dad says. So what's the point? I grow impatient. Son, he says, there are lots of things about work that make no sense. That's what they pay us for, do you see what I mean? More or less, I say.

We park Pedro outside a bar with coloured lights. Dad reminds me to call Mum. I tell him I've just sent her a text. Call her anyway, he insists. Oof. What's great is that afterward he asks the big question: Motel or truck? Truck! I cry, truck! But tomorrow, Dad says pointing a finger at me, we shower, right?

We climb down to take a leak. We brush our teeth using a bottle of water. We make up the bed at the back. We lock the doors. Cover the windows with some strips of plastic. We lie with our backs to the wheel. The bunk is hard. Dad puts his arm round me. His arm smells of sweat and of petrol a bit, too. I like it. When I close my eyes I start hearing the crickets. Don't crickets ever go to sleep?

Elena

They've just left. I hope my son comes back happy. I already know my husband won't be coming back. It was now or never, I agree. Although Mario finds it hard (men do as a rule) to admit that sometimes it's never.

Apart from the possibility of accidents (something which terrifies me even to write), what if he takes a turn for the worse? What if he can't carry on? What would Lito do then? Mario refuses even to contemplate it. He seems convinced that his willpower outstrips his physical strength. As usual I gave in. Not out of generosity, but rather guilt. The absurd thing is that now I regret it all the same.

If Mario accepted the limits of his strength, we would have told all our friends the truth. He prefers us to be secretive. Discreet, he calls it. A patient's rights go unquestioned. No one talks about the rights of the carer. Another person's illness makes us ill. And so I'm in that truck with them, even though I've stayed at home.

Mario insisted he needed to go on a trip with his son at least once in his life. To take him in the truck, the way his father had

done with him. I couldn't refuse him that. But then he came out
with an unacceptable argument. He said that in any event we
could do with the money. Worse: that *I* could do with it. If he's
already putting it like that, then he won't be able to withstand
all those miles. And the fact that he insists on making finan-
cial decisions the way my father-in-law did, like a paterfamilias,
shows that deep down he's in denial about his situation.

I've just called Dr. Escalante. I made an emergency appointment
so that he can tell me about Mario's physical state and whether
he will really make it through this trip. We should have con-
sulted Dr. Escalante before deciding anything. Perhaps Mario
knew what the answer would be, and that's why he was against it
from the start. He kept telling me it was a personal matter, not a
medical one. What was I supposed to do, drag him there? But I
think that now at least I am within my rights to see Dr. Escalante
on my own. I want to know exactly how he found him during
the last checkup. I'm going to ask him to be absolutely honest. I
suppose I must have sounded quite anxious, because he's given
me an appointment tomorrow morning at eleven.

The staff room is not far away, so I'll make the most of it and
go there to prepare the language resits. They are still some way
off, but not working drives me crazy. I'm afraid there are two
kinds of alienation: one is the exploited worker's, the other that of
the worker on holiday. The first has no time to think. The second
can only think, and that is his sentence.

I'm still waiting for Mario to reply to my message. I feel hot
and nervous at the same time. I need to scratch my body hard all
over, until I've peeled away something I can't quite put a name
to. I don't like it when Mario answers the phone while he's

driving. And so I am in his hands. It is me he is throttling as he grips the steering wheel. He turns it. And he is wringing my neck. Enough. I won't continue this diary until I receive his message.

I won't continue this diary until I receive his message.

I won't continue this diary until I receive his message.

I won't continue this diary until. At last, at last.

They are fine. Or so they tell me. At least they were thoughtful enough to send me two messages. Mario's strikes the right note. Concise without being evasive. Affectionate without sounding sentimental. He still knows how to treat me, when he wants. That's what made me fall in love with him: his ability to handle silences as well as words. Some men are brilliant talkers, I've met many like that. But almost none of them know when to be silent. Most of my female friends confuse the tough guys with the silent types. I think that's a movie myth. The worst examples of male aggression I've come across have been intolerably verbal. At full volume.

As usual, I found Lito's reply hard to decipher. All those abbreviations that supposedly speed things up, don't they slow down the meaning of the message? Don't they impede communication? I'm growing old.

I sat in the waiting room for an hour and a half. Seeing all those sick people together didn't exactly put my mind at ease. In the end Dr. Escalante fitted me in between two patients. He gave me no more than five minutes. He nodded practically the whole time and apologized for the rush. When he saw me tormented by all the questions I had, he suggested I come back tomorrow. He has a gap between twelve and twelve-thirty. I'll be there. All he had time to tell me was that, while the trip has its risks, right now Mario's body is experiencing a respite thanks to having stopped taking the drugs. And that this normally boosts the immune system for a limited period. So the additional uplift, although there are no guarantees of course, might help Mario recover some of the strength he lacked months ago. I asked the doctor how limited that period would be. He shrugged and said: Limited.

The cautiousness of doctors irritates me. Conversing with them is like talking on a phone without any coverage. In other words, like listening to yourself speak. They allow you to get things off your chest, to ask questions the answers to which you dread, and gradually to become aware of what's going on based on the information they drip-feed you. Dr. Escalante is a strange man. He knows how to manage his position. He doesn't display his power: he calmly takes it for granted. What strikes me most about him is his air of discreet composure, his aloof self-confidence, combined with the energy of a man his age. I notice that profusion of energy in his look and in his brusque arm movements. As a matter of fact, Dr. Escalante isn't that much younger than I am. And yet when I'm with him, I'm not quite sure why, I feel like an older woman, or as if my life is duller than his. I'll bet anything he doesn't have kids.

Before seeing the doctor, I chatted with Lito and Mario. Lito told me they had slept in the truck. I thought we had agreed they were going to stay in hotels. I chose not to get angry because they seemed happy. Mario told me he hadn't been feeling sick. He sounded relaxed. When he's anxious or he's lying to me, he pauses strangely in mid-sentence; he takes breaths in unnatural places. Lito was shouting excitedly. Hearing him like that comforted me. At the same time it saddened me. He said he saw a landscape just like the one in the Road Runner cartoons. They're eating well. I'm not. I'm going to choose the exam texts. Then I'll spend the afternoon reading. My nerves are calmed by reading. Not true. They aren't calmed, they change direction.

After leaving the surgery, I went (fled) to a bookshop. I bought several novels by authors I like (I chose them quickly, almost without looking, as if I were buying painkillers) and a journal by Juan Gracia Armendáriz, which I leafed through by chance. I suspect his book will be not so much a painkiller as a vaccine: it will inoculate me with the unease I am striving to overcome.

"Illness, like writing, is forced upon us," I underline in the journal, "that is why writers feel awkward when questioned about their condition." In a sense the opposite is true of us teachers, we seem to wear our condition on our sleeve, we exist in a classroom. I imagine the same goes for doctors, only it must be far worse: in the eyes of others, without respite, they are always doctors. "And yet when questioned about their favourite techniques or their best-loved authors, writers will talk incessantly, in the same way the sick become particularly garrulous when we enquire after their ailments," the difference being that writers can't help talking about something that saves them, whereas the sick can't help talking about the thing that is dragging them under.

I have just come from seeing Dr. Escalante. It wasn't what I expected. Not in any sense.

But was I expecting anything?

I arrived at his office exactly on the hour. As I had supposed, I was obliged to wait quite a long time. I was the last to be called in. Dr. Escalante and I greeted one another coldly. He asked me to take a seat. He said, "Let me see," or some such phrase. All perfectly normal. After that, I am not sure what happened, or how.

At first he behaved as always. He listened, nodded, and gave didactic answers, as though avoiding the most troublesome aspect of every reply. That exasperated me, because I hadn't gone back there to revisit platitudes I already know by heart. Sometimes I have the impression doctors tell you things not to help you understand what is happening, but to delay your understanding. Just in case, with any luck, in the meantime the illness is cured. And, if it isn't, at least they will have saved themselves the awkward business of revealing the worst. This cautiousness drives me nuts. I told Dr. Escalante so in no uncertain terms. I detected a look of irony and at the same time of mild satisfaction on his face. He smiled. He seemed to relax. As if he were saying: So you're one of those. The kamikaze type. The type who believe they prefer to know.

At that moment the doctor struck me as a man who knows he is attractive, without being good-looking.

From then on Dr. Escalante's tone changed; he unclasped his hands, moved closer to the edge of his desk. I was immediately on my guard, trying not to straighten my hair, cross my legs, not to blink or anything. And, for the first time, we had an honest conversation. He was brutal, direct, and at the same time respectful toward me. He spoke to me as an equal, without using patronizing euphemisms. He confirmed nearly all my fears.

Although he insisted that the trip wasn't the real problem. I was supposed to know everything he told me, and yet hearing it still shocked me. It made me think of Dr. Escalante as an honourable man. After all, they don't pay him to be that sincere.

When it seemed the conversation was over, one of us, I don't recall who, made some remark about marriage. Nothing memorable. A passing comment. Yet, almost without us realizing it, our conversation was rekindled. And not only did it regain its intensity, it turned more personal. I talked about my son, his uncles, aunts, and grandparents. Escalante spoke of his mother, who died from the same illness he is now attempting to combat. I mentioned the panic attacks that have kept me from sleeping since Mario is the way he is. The doctor confessed that when he first started practising, he suffered from terrible insomnia. And he also told me he was separated. He told me this, I don't know, with unnerving empathy. I pressed myself against the back of my chair. He glanced at the time and frowned. I sprang to my feet and thrust my arm straight out, so as to shake his hand at a distance. He said: I can't believe how late it is. And then, squeezing my hand: I have to go now. I'd gladly ask you along, Elena, but it's a work lunch. I told him not to worry, that I should have left ages ago, that I had to do I don't know what I don't know where. And I hurried toward the door. Then he added: But we could have dinner, if you like.

"I realised what the feeling was that had been besetting me," I underline, as I read a John Banville novel with some trepidation, "since I had stepped that morning into the glassy glare of the consulting rooms," when there is an illness in the family, light angers or even repels us. "It was embarrassment. Embarrassment, yes, a panic-stricken sense of not knowing what to say, where to look, how to behave," until not long ago I loved the mornings, I would get up eager to fill myself with light, and leave for work feeling I was accompanied. Now I prefer the night, which at least has a certain quality of parenthesis, somewhat like a sterile chamber: everything appears slightly deceptive in the dark, nothing seems willing to go on happening. "It was as if a secret had been imparted to us so dirty, so nasty, that we could hardly bear to remain in another's company yet were unable to break free," now Mario is far away but our secret is still here, in the house, "each knowing the foul thing that the other also knew and bound together by that very knowledge," Mario has left, and that knowledge remains. "From that day forward all would be dissembling. There would be no other way to live with death."

Today has been utterly disconcerting. Because I'm not exactly drunk; far from it, I never get drunk, but a little tipsy perhaps. Because it's two in the morning. And because just now, outside the front door, I gave Ezequiel a long hug goodbye and we even brushed the corner of our mouths with our lips. The wine was wonderful, made entirely from grapes harvested at night, or so the sommelier told us, what all of them? Amazing, how can they possibly see the grapes? Truly wonderful, I wrote down the name of the vineyard so that I can order some online, it wasn't too tart or too fruity, the sommelier was terribly friendly.

Maybe some coffee will clear my head.

✧ ✧ ✧

In fact, I entered the restaurant determined to tell him I wasn't going to have dinner with him. That I had thought better of it and regretted the misunderstanding. Of course, it would have been easier to tell him over the phone. But, as it turned out, I didn't have his private number or his e-mail address. The doctor, I mean Ezequiel, it still feels strange calling him that, had hurriedly proposed dinner. He had named a restaurant, a street, a time. And had virtually run away. I scarcely nodded. I didn't refuse, that was all. I stood dazed outside the office door. It had a sign on it with the full names of all the different specialists and their working hours. His were finished for the day. That was the first time I had paid any attention to his first name. I should call off that dinner. Then I realized I had no way of getting hold of him outside the office. Was that a strategic omission on his part? I don't think so. But, in short, I had to turn up at the restaurant. It would have been rude to simply stand him up. Him of all people. My husband's doctor.

How embarrassing, my God, how embarrassing.

Not only that. I even arrived ten minutes early. And he was already in the restaurant. He told me he had had to check on a patient, and as he lived relatively close by, he had decided to wait for me there. I was wrong-footed, because to leave suddenly in that situation would have been like saying: Then you've waited in vain, goodbye. What I really wanted was to have arrived first. Seen him come in. Greeted him politely, making it perfectly clear I had taken the trouble to wait for him. Apologized. Paid for my drink and left. That is what I had imagined. But Ezequiel stood up to greet me, he looked very pleased to see me, he was extremely attentive, he told me he had just ordered a bottle of Merlot rarely found in our country. And so I said nothing, sat down, and smiled like an idiot.

From then on everything that happened, how can I put it? acted like an antidote. Every word, every gesture conspired to block my path and prevent my escape. Ezequiel could have avoided talking about Mario (a clumsy move that would have vexed me and driven me instantly from the table), but he did precisely the opposite. He mentioned him from the very beginning, incorporating him into the conversation so naturally that it felt almost as though my husband had arranged the dinner himself but had been unable to come at the last minute. Ezequiel could also have asked me overly personal questions, as though imposing intimacy upon me. But he behaved in exactly the opposite way; he was discreet about my life and extremely open about his own. After we ordered the second bottle, Ezequiel could have made overtures, subtly in any case (which at that point I would still have bridled at somewhat), yet he didn't make the least move. Not even to glance at my cleavage. Which, although nothing to write home about, was nevertheless there.

Now that I come to think of it, a man only achieves such a level of restraint if that is what he has set out to do. I mean, only if it is premeditated. My God. In any case, it's too late now. Not because we have done anything irreparable. But because it's past four in the morning and I am wide awake. And because I was incapable of telling Ezequiel when I arrived at the restaurant, or during the meal, or as we walked back to the house, or when I heard him say his phone number, that it had all been a mistake, that I would never call him, that I didn't want to see him. That much is irreparable. Almost as irreparable as having written *my God* so many times. Such an atheist and so drunk.

I look out of the window and I don't know what to do. Whether to lean out and yell, throw myself head first onto the pavement, or hail a cab.

✧ ✧ ✧

"She was also something of a feminist, not crazy," I underline in one of Cynthia Ozick's short stories, "but she resented having 'Miss' put in front of her name; she thought it pointedly discriminatory, she wanted to be a lawyer among lawyers." The pupils call us female teachers *Miss* or, at worst, *Ms*. If it comes to that I'd prefer harassment. "Though she was no virgin she lived alone." What fun *Miss* Ozick has. I remember once, during a dinner, a man asked my sister if she lived alone. In a rare show of humour, my sister replied: Yes, I'm married.

Why did I lack the courage to pursue my academic career? Admittedly, the precariousness alarmed me, finding myself on the street at thirty, being the umpteenth jobless researcher, *et alia*. But there was something else. Something around me I could see rather more clearly than my dubious vocation.

Having observed the fate of my former women colleagues, I consider myself sufficiently well-informed to sketch this brief

PERVERSE OUTLINE
OF THE
ASPIRING FEMALE ACADEMIC

to be expanded upon below, esteemed gentlemen of the panel, in the hope that it displays some aptitude for synthesis:

YOU ARE CAPABLE
~~YOU ARE INCAPABLE~~

[*id est:* you're dumb]

YOU ARE CAPABLE AND HOT
~~YOU ARE CAPABLE AND NOT HOT~~
[id est: you're ugly]

YOU ARE CAPABLE, HOT, AND YOU LET MEN
LOOK AT YOUR TITS
~~YOU ARE CAPABLE, HOT, AND YOU DON'T LET~~
~~MEN LOOK AT YOUR TITS~~
[id est: you're a prude]

YOU ARE CAPABLE, HOT, YOU LET MEN LOOK
AT YOUR TITS, AND THEY PROMOTE YOU
~~YOU ARE CAPABLE, HOT, YOU LET MEN LOOK~~
~~AT YOUR TITS, AND THEY DON'T PROMOTE~~
~~YOU~~
[id est: you're a slut]

YOU ARE CAPABLE, HOT, YOU LET MEN LOOK
AT YOUR TITS, THEY PROMOTE YOU, AND YOU
SPEND YOUR WHOLE LIFE SHOWING YOUR
GRATITUDE TO YOUR MENTOR
~~YOU ARE CAPABLE, HOT, YOU LET MEN LOOK~~
~~AT YOUR TITS, THEY PROMOTE YOU, AND YOU~~
~~DON'T SPEND YOUR WHOLE LIFE SHOWING~~
~~YOUR GRATITUDE TO YOUR MENTOR~~
[id est: you're ungrateful]

YOU ARE CAPABLE, HOT, YOU LET MEN LOOK
AT YOUR TITS, THEY PROMOTE YOU, YOU
SPEND YOUR WHOLE LIFE SHOWING YOUR
GRATITUDE TO YOUR MENTOR, AND, VERY

IMPROBABLY, YOU TAKE OVER HIS POST WHEN
HE RETIRES
~~YOU ARE CAPABLE, HOT, YOU LET MEN LOOK~~
~~AT YOUR TITS, THEY PROMOTE YOU, YOU~~
~~SPEND YOUR WHOLE LIFE SHOWING YOUR~~
~~GRATITUDE TO YOUR MENTOR, AND, OF~~
~~COURSE, YOU RETIRE HAVING NEVER TAKEN~~
~~OVER HIS POST~~

[*id est:* you're over the hill]

We trust this has not wearied you, esteemed gentlemen of the panel, and that our research will attain, if not your unmerited theoretical approval, then at least your paternal consent to carry on failing. Thank you very much.

I take my phone out of my bag, I turn it on, look at it, leave it on the table, put it back in my bag, take it out again. I act like a delinquent.

The first thing I did when I got up was call Mario. It took a while to get hold of him. They seem fine. They are seeing places, enjoying themselves. They sound almost happier without me. When I asked Mario whether he was sleeping eight hours a day like he had promised, he hesitated. I got annoyed and we argued. We fell silent. And then we were tender. Lito tried to explain something to me about the truck and the rain, I couldn't hear very well, whatever it was it sounded adorable. He told me very excitedly that he had beaten his dad in a race. I asked him to let me speak to Mario again. He promised he hadn't really run, how could I even think that, didn't I know the little tyke had an overactive imagination. We ended on a happy note. I felt reassured. I busied myself cleaning windows. I did some washing. I boiled vegetables. I read for a while. I prepared the literature exams. I sewed on two buttons. Then I called Ezequiel.

He asked me if I had thought about our dinner the previous night. I said no. He asked me if I'd had difficulty getting to sleep. I said no. He suggested meeting for coffee this afternoon. I said no. He asked if he could call me tomorrow. I said yes.

"Hypocrite lecteuse! Ma semblable! Ma sœur!," I underline with a highlighter in a manifesto by Margaret Atwood, hypocrisy is a leveller, sisterly hypocrisy, sister hypocrisy, "Let us now praise stupid women," praise them, praise them!, "who have given us Literature." Without stupid women, not a single love poem would have ever been written.

Is Mario jealous? Somewhat. Am I jealous? Not particularly.

I could just as well have written: Is he jealous? Not really, because he acknowledges it as such. Because he is a man at ease with his jealousy. Like my sister is with hers. She even cultivates it. She regards jealousy as a sign of love.

And I could as well have written: Am I jealous? Perhaps in a twisted way. Because, although in theory I am less possessive than they are, in fact I am afraid to acknowledge the possessive impulse in myself.

Is jealousy related to love? It is related: they fight. They probably cancel each other out. Are fantasies related to marriage?

They are related: they cohabit. Maybe they are mutually sustaining.

Not long ago I reached a certain age, how can I define it? an age: that's all. After which we begin counting it, we become too aware of it. It isn't a number so much as a kind of frontier.

Why is it that suddenly, without having decided to, we begin noticing younger people? Observing them with a certain nervousness? Why are we tempted to attract their attention, to display ourselves surreptitiously in front of them? What do we hope they will avoid? What do we want them to give us back?

Any woman who thinks this is a problem restricted to men, very well: she is probably naïve, a coward, or a hypocrite. I have women friends who fit neatly into all three categories. Until one day, when they least expect it, they leave their bald husbands for some other man.

I can't help but admit that I, too, am turning into That. The thing I didn't want to become. I should have been fully prepared. I had seen it in books, films, in my neighbours. But that couldn't happen to me. Yet it has: I am starting to mistake beauty for youth.

Mario

. . . testing, testing, let's see, is this piece of shit working or not?, testing, tes, well, it seems to be, getting started is difficult, breathing is a bit of a struggle sometimes, but the main thing is to get started, isn't it?, like with Pedro, after that, well, everything speeds up, I'll explain, bah, can I explain this?, you're at your grandparents' and you don't know why, we've sent you there until the end of the holidays, I'm meant to be travelling, we talk every day, I try to sound cheerful, am I deceiving you, son?, yes, I'm deceiving you, am I doing the right thing?, I've no idea, so let's assume I am, I prefer you not to see me like this, we can't tell you what's going on now, what is now in any case, if I don't even know when you're listening to me, will those mp thingamajigs still exist?, or will iPods seem as old-fashioned to your kids as my record player?, formats disappear just like people, hold on, is this thing still recor—.

And at the same time I'm not sure, do you see?, I swear I'd give my life to, how ironic is that, I'd give anything to know what's going to happen to this lie, what you'll think of me when you discover it, you'll have a few photos of me, I hope, and if so you'll look at them sometimes, won't you?, but I have no way of seeing you, I mean, will you be a nice guy or a rogue?, or will you be nice some of the time and a bit of a bastard others, like the rest of us?, and, you know, I try, I really do try to figure out if you're going to look like me, not too much I trust, for your sake, and part of me is desperate for you to grow up now, and another part of me is scared by how fast you, I mean, for you time will also, well, and I spend hours inventing a face, a height for you, but not a voice, I can't do voices, it's strange, I make up bodies, but I remember voices, and I can picture your back, your nose, whatever, your beard, you have a beard?, I can't believe it.

Let's say that with you I've had good intentions but not much initiative, I fooled myself into believing I was waiting, waiting for you, for instance, the last few summers you'd been asking me if you could go with Uncle Juanjo on a delivery, he suggested it, he told me, but your mother and I were never sure, we thought it was dangerous, or not right for your age, or heck knows what, there'll be time, we said, we thought there'd be plenty, and suddenly, or not so suddenly, there wasn't any, that's why I had to do it like this, in such a hurry, I had to create this memory for you, your mum was against it at first, we argued quite a lot, I was feeling better, and you know those trips, the ones the travel agency was supposedly sending me on?, well, I was staying with your uncle and aunt for a few days, until I had recovered a bit from the side effects, then I came home and did the best I could, your mother, it goes without saying—wait, someone's coming in.

Once I quit taking the poison there was a, like a kind of illusion, I had mornings when I was elated, I got up and thought: I'm cured, then the next day I returned to reality, I had ups and downs, and during one of these remissions I asked Uncle Juanjo what deliveries he had, are you sure? he said, are you sure?, then I suggested we go together, that came first, right?, and at the same time, why not, it would bring in some money, the pay was good, and I, well, you'll agree, son, I was thinking about how little money we had left in the bank, about the mortgage payments, needing a new car, things like that, and I had a duty to you, didn't I?, your duty is to take care of your health, your mother said, but this summer it was different, I hardly felt sick at all, you'd just had your birthday, the delivery date was okay, you can tell there aren't as many truckers to put the screws on during the holidays, damned bloodsuckers, I more or less knew the route, I'd been there once with your granddad, he was the one who started trucking, then Uncle Juanjo took over, bah, and I was supposed to, that's another story, your granddad wanted it to be me, you know?, he even taught me how to move trailers, how to strip engines, how to budget, I don't know why the heck we teach our kids to behave the way we do, when we know we aren't happy, sometimes when I think about it, I swear I—

Yesterday I didn't feel so good, I tried to take a nap, then your mum came back, I had a bad night, bah, we both did, I've been thinking a lot lately about when she and I met, it's amazing to think we might have lived different lives, a life without the other, the first thing I did after I told your granddad I was leaving the company was to enrol at the university, and it was a big shock for him, you know?, my father was one of those men who chop cheese with one stroke, you know?, that's where I met your mum, she didn't take much notice of me at first, how can I put it, she was more interested in rich kids, she denies it, we never agree about that part of the story, then luckily she started taking more of an interest in the lousy students, I had spotted her from day one, long before we started dating, do people still say *dating*?, maybe I sound old-fashioned, your mum would get straight A's, you know what she's like, heaven forbid a B, I used to scrape through, I never went near a classroom, as soon as I found out your mum wrote short stories I quickly did some research, oh yes, dear, I crammed for that all right, it's called doing field work.

Well, and that's how she and I got started, I would tell her half jokingly: I'm your consolation prize, it irritated her, but I guess it was kind of true, her family always thought so, I didn't care, we met up every day, lent each other books, went halves on buying records, studied together, well, not that so much, we went camping, the whole shebang, until midway through my degree I got this feeling, I don't know, of being trapped, finally I decided to take a year off and go travelling, I went all over with my backpack, stopping at any old place, I got money from wherever I could, doing odd jobs, borrowing, or if I had to, well, I even read more books, I tell you, in hostels, in parks, in van—no, thanks, I still have some, yes, thanks.

I came back in the summer, and your mother said we should move in together, how about that? move in together or never see each other again, she told me, I was flabbergasted, we'd spoken hundreds of times on the phone, exchanged heaps of letters, but, I don't know, I think during that year she tried a different life as well, and different men, she says she didn't, and we both went off, to live together, I mean, and your mum got her degree, and never applied for that research grant, to tell the truth, that suited me fine, I preferred her to get a steady teaching job, now I'm not so sure, I don't know, around that time, more or less, is when she stopped writing, in the meantime I had to do something, of course, I wasn't about to go back to studying, and I wasn't going to hang around waiting for my in-laws to give me a handout, in short, I started to look for things related to travelling, I did this and that, and then I started working at the travel agency, I was used to moving around, not to dealing with tourists, a tourist, you might say, is someone who pays you in order not to move around, at first I thought of it as a stopgap, it was convenient, near home, finding something better wasn't so easy, you know?, and so I stayed on, I began to settle, and the years went by like crazy, my parents died, one then the other, just imagine, as if they'd made a pact, your grandma always longed to have grandchildren, how can I describe her to you? my mother walked around staring down at her feet, the more they yelled at her at home, the more she painted her nails, and Uncle Juanjo took over the company, he was always telling me: why don't you come and work with me, you know you love the open road, but we'd just had you, Lito, and something strange started happening to me, I started to be afraid of the open road, and every time that I . . .

Lito

We arrive at Veracruz de los Aros and then it happens again. The sky clouds over. All at once. First I thought it was a fluke. No. No way. I've done loads of tests. And it works. If I concentrate really hard, the weather changes. I don't know who has the power. Pedro or me. But it's true. Maybe that's why they gave the truck that name, Wasn't he the saint who carried round the keys of heaven? I was worried that Dad might laugh at me and all that. I know him so well. I'm glad he takes me much more seriously now. That's the good thing about being ten and sharing a truck. So I told him about my discovery. Dad tested it too. And he saw it was true.

It depends on my mood. If everything's okay, it's sunny. If I get bored, it clouds over a bit. When I'm restless, it gets windy. If I get angry and cry, it rains. The other day, for instance, Dad was furious because I stuck my arms out of the window. It scares me when Dad bawls at me like that. And that night there was lightning. Of course, you have to be patient. The sky won't change as soon as I think of it. It's like Dad says: You have to drive a long way to travel a short distance. But if I keep it up, eventually it happens. Like mealtimes.

I send a text from Dad's phone:

```
hi ma hw r u? we r awsm! saw ++s of grt plcs 2day
dt wrry dad nt drvg fst :-) xxxs luv u
```

Mum replies:

```
Thank you my darling for your delicious message.
Your mum is fine but she misses you loads. Be
careful climbing in and out of Pedro. I went
swimming today. You are my angel, kiss Daddy
for me.
```

Mum doesn't know how to use the phone, I laugh. What do you mean? Dad says, she uses it every day. And she had one before you were born, grumpy arthropod. Sure, I say, but she doesn't know. Her messages always have twenty or thirty letters too many. It's more expensive. And she wastes about a hundred letters. There are some things you don't skimp on, Dad says. And you, I go on, don't know how to use it either. Oh, heck, pardon me, he says, why? Let's see, I say, where in the menu do you find the games? That's unfair, he complains. Ask me about something I might have a use for. Okay, okay, I say. How do you copy your contacts list? He doesn't say anything. You see? I say. Then I raise my arms and whoop like I'd just scored a goal. Arthropod! says Dad.

We stop at another service station. Dad keeps wanting me to take a leak. Like I was an eight- or nine-year-old. He says it's not good to hold it in. That it's best to go right at the start. And, because we drink so much Coke, in the end I always go a bit. We climb out. The sun blinds me. Dad is wearing shades. He points to some metal doors. I crinkle my nose to try to see them. Last one to the toilet cleans Pedro's windows, I shout. Dad smiles and shakes his head. You're afraid I'll win, right? I try saying. I'm afraid the effort will make you wet yourself before you get there, he replies. Liar! Liar! I accuse him. Pants on fire! he teases. Don't be a spoilsport, I complain. Don't you be so competitive, he says. I stop walking. I lift my head. I put my hand over my eyebrows and say: Please, please, please. Dad stands still. He sighs. He looks ahead of him. He grips his belt. He sighs again. You count, he whispers. One, two! I shout. After that all I hear is the sound made by the soles of my trainers.

I reach the door to the toilet. Me. First. For a moment I think Dad may have let me win. That always annoys me. This time it's different. Because he actually ran and he's all shaken up. It's true Dad had that virus last year. And he still isn't the same as before. He says he is. I know he isn't. But his belly isn't so big. So he should be quicker than when he was fat. I don't know. I beat him anyway. This summer is so cool. As soon as school starts I'm going to take on that jerk Martin Alonso, who always beats me at races. I leave the toilet. Dad doesn't. It takes him quite a long time these days. But when I take just a bit long, he grumbles. Although. I'm not surprised considering what comes out. Dad shits a lot and it's hard. I've seen it. Finally he appears. His face and T-shirt are soaked. Good idea. Me too.

We cross Sierra Juárez. Dad can't find the radio station he likes. So he lets me choose the music. I'm happy and it's getting warmer. Further proof of Pedro's power. I've thought a lot about it and I've realized that it's him. Or rather, it's the two of us. For it to work the truck has to be moving and I have to be on board. Dad looks at the map the whole time. Are you okay? he asks. Great, I reply. We should be in Fuentevaca by now, he says. Pedro's tired so he's going more slowly, I laugh. Papa doesn't find it funny. His jokes are worse. I switch on the phone to play for a bit. I choose mini-golf. I still don't understand the rules. But I keep scoring more and more points. Lito, Dad says, I think we'd better spend the night at a motel, right? I think there's one near here. We need to take a shower. And to get a good night's sleep. Because tomorrow (the ball spins round in a weird way, it gets bigger, flies up like it's coming out of the screen, disappears, the yardage calculator keeps going, the trees lean a bit to the right, the crosswind makes the shot more difficult, the ball appears, then grows smaller again, falls in slo-mo, bounces once, twice, three times, keeps rolling slower and slower, what would it be like to play in the hills?, is there such a thing as mountain golf?, the ball lands on the green, skips closer, the flag's in sight, what a shot, ladies and gentlemen!, it rolls a few feet further, no, I don't think it's going to make it), hey, son, hey, are you listening to me or not? Yes, yes, I reply.

The motel is full of old junk. There's a smell of fish coming from the back. The guy at reception has gaps in his teeth. He wears his shirt half open. His chest is all sunburned. He looks like a thug. Dad gives him some money. The thug hands us the key. Not a card. A proper key with a key ring and all. A round, heavy key ring. Like a golf ball. Do you have Internet? I ask. The thug's gums go even pinker. What do you think, kid? he replies. Come along, son, come along, Dad puts an arm round me. The dining room's at the back. Sure. At the back. Where the fish are rotting.

I make bread pellets. I roll them on the tablecloth. I flick

them with my middle finger. I try to aim them between the water jug and the breadbasket. The pellets slide fast because the
tablecloth is oilskin. So far I've scored nine goals and had six
misses. Could be better. Don't you like the soup? Dad asks. He
looks sad as he says this. So I tell a lie. Dad cheers up a bit. I put
another spoonful in my mouth. This soup should be used in
chemical warfare. They could fire it from tubes out of light air-
craft. And everyone would die. I shoot two more pellets. One
goes in, one goes out. I play one more to make it the best of
three. Good shot. Dad puts a white pill on the tip of his tongue.
Then he smiles. I get a bit carsick on those mountain roads, he
explains, too many bends. I saw him take the exact same pill
yesterday. And there weren't as many bends as today. I look at
the man at the opposite table. The dining-room light is far away,
so it looks as if he only has half a face. Maybe the other half is
missing. Maybe he ate up all his soup and it's disintegrated. Suddenly the man with half a face sees I'm looking at him. And he
stares straight at me. But his face doesn't move. Not even an
inch.

There's a rusty fan on the ceiling. The fan makes me a bit nervous. It goes round and round. It wobbles a lot. And it's nearer to
my side. I ask Dad if he'll swap beds with me. Dad says no. Then
he tickles me and we swap. I turn on the TV. It's teeny. I channel
surf. On one Stallone is twisting the arm of a big fat man. I've
seen that film before. It's awesome. On another there's the presi-
dent with a gaggle of microphones. On another the police are
firing tear gas. On another there are naked women. Dad tells
me to change the channel. On another there's a football match I
don't know where. The players' names are really weird. On
another there's a woman skater bouncing off the ice in slo-mo.
He switches the light off. I don't feel sleepy yet. I ask if I can go

on watching TV for a bit. He says yes but with the sound off. I tell him it's no fun watching TV with the sound off. He says it's no fun with it on either. Then he gives a big yawn. And he takes a sleeping pill. I turn the TV off. Dad says: Goodnight speedy chelonian. Wasn't I an arthropod today? I ask. That was yesterday, he replies, it's after midnight.

Elena

I was going to say he drives me wild. But besides being cheesy, that would be inaccurate. It's more like, with Ezequiel as a pretext, through his body, I had allowed myself to go wild. His healthy young body. Distant from death.

As I write this I despise myself, but sometimes Mario's body disgusts me. Touching it is as difficult for me as it is for him to look at himself in the mirror. His scaly skin. His bony frame. His flaccid muscles. His sudden baldness. I was prepared for us to grow old together, not for this. Not to go to sleep next to a man my age and wake up next to someone prematurely old. Whom I continue to love. Whom I no longer desire.

I know what I'm doing is wretched. I suppose I am going to feel extreme remorse. Good. Everything is extreme. Because now, tonight, all I could feel was bestial, unforgivable pleasure. Tomorrow I don't know. And the day after tomorrow I'll be dead.

Ezequiel's power can't be appreciated when you see him naked. He has to be seen in movement. Gesticulating, approaching, assaulting. His physique is a refutation of the platonic. He is

audacious, not muscular. Intense, not athletic. What is irresist-
ible is his conviction. Which encourages me to overlook my own
defects. This is essential when in bed with a man. Not what I see
in his body: what he can make me see in mine. When I am with
Ezequiel, I adore myself. I concentrate on our actions. And our
actions are all, *my God*.

I remember early on, when we were very young, feeling in-
timidated by Mario. His robustness. His symmetry. I had never
been confronted by such a beautiful nude. But, in bed, I couldn't
give myself fully. I didn't find disorder. It was like embracing the
treasure chest and being unable to open it. I hoped that things
would improve by living together. And they did improve, but not
very much. Now I think that deep down, because it seemed to
me his body was more admirable than mine, I was constantly
wriggling away, choosing my best side, half-posing. With Ezequiel I allow myself to be plain. Vulgar. Ugly. Excitingly ugly.

I need to touch myself. Or I will keep going round in circles,
without ever getting to the point.

Good. Okay. The point.

Ezequiel doesn't fit any of the categories catered by the
porn industry. His tastes are different. He likes zits. Dirty heels.
Rippling flab. Hairs sprouting everywhere. Like the ones that
resemble pinheads embedded in the groin. He even likes farts.
It's quite extraordinary. Anything that can be smelled, sucked,
squeezed or bitten hard, he considers worthy of the greatest
admiration. He chews my armpits. He licks my unshaven legs.
He sucks my feet where my sandals have rubbed the skin raw.
He smells my anus. He rubs his cock against the roughness on

my elbows. He comes on my stretch marks. He says that all this, my wealth of imperfections, comes from health itself.

Today, at his place, he explained that every day he sees so many bodies shrivelling up, losing their glow, degenerating pore by pore, that he has started to be excited by what is most alive, everything that flows with eagerness out of the body. To him, beauty is exactly that.

While we were talking I stood up, naked, in front of the wardrobe mirror. Still sweating slightly, Ezequiel, remained lying down, hands clasped behind his head. His feet were crossed, and he was looking at me looking at myself. I examined everything I most hate about my body. My lopsided nipples. The scar from my caesarean. That sagging flesh on my inner thigh. That loathsome puffiness above my knees. My too-broad calves. The perennial corns on my little toes. Then I observed myself from the side. I focused on the folds of my stomach. On my diminished buttocks, which look as if the muscles have been absorbed to the sides. On the dwindling roundness of my breasts as they become more elongated and hollow. Sock boobs, my sister and I used to call them when we made fun of old women. I thought I looked rather repulsive. And for once I didn't care.

I confessed to Ezequiel that for a couple of years now, I have had a penchant for looking at myself in the mirror too much. I spend the same amount of time looking in it as when I was a teenager. I often find myself scrutinizing my naked body, reflecting on whether it might still be considered desirable. I asked him whether he thought that was wrong. On the contrary, he said. We ought to look at ourselves every day. See how we are in decline, losing our shape, how our skin is starting to grow rougher. And that only in this way can we understand and accept the passage of time.

His response seemed to me a little too unpleasant. And not very seductive. And that what he was actually saying, playing the scientist, was that I am old. I was offended. I insulted him. I became aroused. Then he insulted me. Then he penetrated me up against the wardrobe mirror. Then I wept. Then I thanked him.

I spent the entire day fretting because Mario didn't answer the phone. Finally he got back to me. They stopped at Comala de la Vega and are now on their way to Región. Lito told me he knows how to guess the number of inhabitants. And that he misses me. And that he wants a Valentino something-or-other wristwatch. Mario says he feels fine, just a little tired. He spoke to me in that tone of forced calm he adopts when he doesn't want me to interrogate him. I wanted to know if he had vomited and he feigned surprise. I'm not Lito, I reminded him, and I'm not stupid either. Then he admitted he had, twice. And changed the subject. It drives me crazy when Mario assumes that controlling attitude of his. As though illness depended on our level of composure. Mario is brave, his brothers keep repeating like parrots. If he were as brave as all that, he would weep with me each time we speak.

At one point during the call, Mario asked me how I was. And, he added and I quote, what I was getting up to. It was an innocent question. I think. I had a mental block. I felt a lump in my throat. And I had to pretend I was losing coverage.

"There's a lot of horribleness she refuses to countenance," I agree with what Helen Garner writes in one of her novels, "but it won't just go away." In fact the job of horror is to do the opposite: to resurface. "So somebody else has to sort of live it." By avoiding the subject of his death, Mario delegates it to me, he kills me a little. "Death will not be denied. To try is grandiose." And feeds it. "It drives madness into the soul." Like one truck driving into another. "It leaches out virtue." Leaves it barren. "And makes a mockery of love." And there are no more clean embraces. Here all of us fall ill.

Lito sent me a wonderful e-mail from Salto Grande. With his comma-free sentences, his strange spelling. I miss him as never before, in a way that feels more like physical pain than affection. I feel ransacked inside. As though all the energy I normally spend on my adorable and unruly son had been extinguished due to the absence of any recipient. People who don't have kids think they suck you dry (which they do, I swear), but they don't realize that this energy, which our kids guzzle down like water from a canteen, is the exact same one we stole from them. It is like a two-way circuit. Without Lito here I work less but get more tired. The only thing that recharges my batteries is having sex with Ezequiel.

"Two-way circuit?" "Recharge my batteries?" All of a sudden I am talking like Mario. As though language were taking revenge on me.

Bringing up a child and caring for a sick person have this in common: both require an energy that is not really yours. You are instilled with it by them, by their eager love, their expectant fear. And they clamour for it as though scenting fresh meat. I sometimes feel that motherhood is a black hole. Whatever you put in is never enough, and you've no idea where it goes. At other times, though, I feel like a vampire feeding off her own child. Devouring his enthusiasm in order to carry on believing in life.

But a child is also a deposit box. However selfish that may sound, you invest in him your time, your sacrifices, your expectations, in the hope that in the future he will yield gratitude. I argued about this with my sister, who called me again yesterday. She asked about Mario and told me she was looking for a flight. I told her not to worry, and that I know how busy she is with work at this time of year. I'm actually dying for her to come. As always, we ended up talking about our respective families. We never talk about ourselves. I told her a child is literally an investment. She said that was a horrible idea. That motherhood couldn't be understood in economic terms. And that whatever I do I should never say such a thing to Lito. It wouldn't be so bad. Kids also speculate with their love, they spend their lives making mundane calculations: if I'm good today, I'll get this; if I'm bad I'll get that taken away; if I'm nice to Dad I'll have a few days worth of credit; if I'm nice to Mum the two of us can negotiate with him. That's how we are.

Day after day you put the best (and the worst) of yourself into your child. And in the meantime you wonder: Will he notice? Will he remember? Will it do him any good? And, because you are no saint, you also wonder: Will he acknowledge it? Will he reward me for it? Will he want to look after me?

I wonder whether, perhaps without realizing it, we seek out the books we need to read. Or whether books themselves, which are intelligent entities, detect their readers and catch their eye. In the end, every book is the *I Ching*. You pick it up, open it and there it is, there you are.

In a novel by Mario Levrero, I'm startled when I recognize a familiar idea. The fact that the author and my husband share the same name has an even greater impact on my memory. The main character is stretched out beside his lover. He senses she doesn't want to make love with him. And so he simply lies there on his back and takes her hand in his. She sighs with relief. And lays her head on his chest. Then the two of them experience an instant of complete communion, beyond the sexual realm or perhaps coming after the sexual realm: "I could be more graphic by saying we had a child that night, born not of flesh but of the denial of the flesh. And I sometimes shudder to think it may still be alive in its own world, doing who knows what. And yet I sense it was an ephemeral being."

I remember when Mario didn't want to have kids, or wasn't sure he wanted them. We were just starting out and we thought our solitude was enough to fill the house. We spent whole afternoons simply clutching one another or holding hands, gazing out of the window. Whenever we spoke about it, Mario would tell me that we were our own child. That we cared for one another, nurtured one another. We felt we had created something attached to the two of us. That kind of creature who was both of us when we were together.

In the end we were three. The house filled up. And something, I am not sure what exactly, was driven out from between us.

As we become more confident in bed, Ezequiel begins to reveal himself. My initial response was instinctive rejection. I almost forbade him ever to touch me again. With his first attempt we screamed at each other. Not true: I did all the screaming. He remained calm. He didn't even get up as I was putting my clothes on. He went on talking to me slowly, in that anaesthetizing tone he has. Lying among the pillows. Smiling, naked. With a slightly lopsided erection.

Angry, I asked him if by any chance he took me for a sadomasochist. Ezequiel merely replied: If you were in my line of work, sadomasochism would seem the most natural thing in the world.

After recovering from my initial shock, I couldn't help thinking about everything that lay in store for me. That in any event I hadn't much to lose, or rather that I couldn't lose much more than I already had. I felt again the way I did the first night we spent together, when Ezequiel admired my composure in dealing with the situation and said to me: I can't take my eyes off your breasts or your dignity.

I agreed with trepidation. Just this once. To give it a try. As long as he promised to stop the moment I felt uncomfortable. That's what we did. That's what he did to me.

It didn't take me long to realize that it was exactly what I needed. To reclaim my body. All of it, not just a part of it. An unmitigated punishment. A pain that would awaken me.

So now I am awakening.

He wants to hit me and wants me to hit him. He asks me to penetrate him with all kinds of household objects. The more threatening they look, the more they appeal to him. Ezequiel suggests we do things that, until only recently, I would have considered reportable. He collects ghastly films that arouse me in ways I later feel ashamed of. He dreams up forms of masturbation where we suffer simultaneously. He takes me from feeling ticklish to panic, from panting to pleading. As we thrash about he insults me in a way that ought to revolt me. His fixation on my anus reaches extremes I had never imagined. I don't mean penetration (we already tried that, with remarkable roughness, during our second meeting), but unexpected explorations involving all five senses. I say all five because, as well as seeing, touching, biting, and smelling everything, Ezequiel (I am serious) listens to my flesh. I had never seen, or of course heard, of this before. He does it on any part of my body. He lays his cheek against my skin, his ear up close, like a gynaecologist monitoring contractions, and narrows his eyes. And he smiles. I don't know what he is hearing.

Tradition has it that sex results in the little death. I now believe that those who say this haven't experienced the pleasure of harm. Because with Ezequiel I find the opposite is true: each fuck results in a resurrection. We insult each other. We tear into each other. We cause each other pain in order to make sure we are still here. And each time we reaffirm the other's presence, the other's suffering, we are as moved as if it were a reunion. Then I have orgasms that stretch the limits of my existence. As though my existence were a vaginal muscle.

I want to avenge myself on my own flesh.

The protagonist of a Richard Ford novel watches his lover in bed. He finds her distant or disappointed. I highlight his speculation: "Maybe that isn't even surprising when you come down to it, since by scaling down my own pleasures I may have sold short her hopes for herself."

It's true, pleasure brings hope. Maybe that is why so many men leave us dissatisfied: their desire holds no promise. They are wary when they get into bed. As though they were already leaving before they have arrived. We women, even if only for a moment, even if we aspire to nothing more, tend to give ourselves completely, out of instinct or habit.

That is what makes Ezequiel so unusual. He gives himself, he squeezes himself dry, he pushes you to the limits. And it is obvious he never expects anything in return.

As a woman you often let yourself go and you don't even know why. The men you sleep with don't know either. It usually surprises or intimidates them. As though, with the expansion of your own pleasure, you were demanding something from them. Not that I blame them. We women are one long affliction. Perhaps that is why we are good at caring for the sick: we identify with their demanding side. Perhaps that is why men make such ham-fisted nurses. Filth terrifies them because they feel implicated by it. We women seem to like getting soiled. With discharge, blood, shit, anything. Poor us, poor them. If I could choose, I would be a man. And I would never get soiled without asking why.

I still can't decide whether Ezequiel is masterfully cynical or a monster of empathy. Every night, after eating together, we talk about Mario. With infinite patience he describes the progress of the disease, the secondary problems in other organs, the general state of his immune system. He is careful to sum up the facts and to find instructive examples so he can be sure I understand. At such moments I find it hard to feel I am cheating, because this feels like a home visit. Ezequiel refers to palliative care with such tact, he speaks of my husband with such respect, that I begin to wonder whether he even considers our relationship inappropriate, let alone deviant. As though, in the meticulous Dr. Escalante's eyes, caring for his patients involved the carnal duty of attending to their wives.

After clarifying my medical doubts, he lets me unburden

myself. He watches me weep from just the right distance: not too close (so as not to be intrusive) not too far (so as not to abandon me). At this stage he refrains from intervening. He simply watches me and from time to time gives a faint smile. I would even venture to say there is a measure of love in his silence. An unhealthy love perhaps, one permeated with the substance he is dealing with. When I can weep no more, I am assailed by a sense of exposure. Then Ezequiel comes to my aid, offers me warmth, embraces me, kisses my hair, whispers in my ear, caresses me, squeezes me, sticks his tongue in my mouth, undresses me, scratches me, rubs himself against me, tears my underwear, bites me between my thighs, pins down my arms, penetrates me, violates me, consoles me.

I think about the orgasms I am having. Not better or longer. Simply different in kind. Radiating from new places. I was convinced I had never experienced anything like it, until just now when I remembered something that may have been a precursor: the sad, quiet, tender fuck Mario and I had the day we found out what his illness was. Almost the last, in fact. Since then we have scarcely wanted or known how to make love amid so much death. On that occasion I had an anomalous orgasm. Like it belonged to some other woman. Perhaps this is where it all started. It sounds grotesque, but besides the sorrow we both shared it aroused me to imagine that the body penetrating me and making me come was fading, was almost a ghost.

That night there was a storm. It rained with a vengeance. There were loud claps of thunder. Trees swayed and objects banged about. We heard it all from the bedroom while we were making love. During the final moment I felt suspended. I was able to think with complete lucidity. Or rather I contemplated ideas that came unbidden. As Mario began to ejaculate, I could picture myself fixed in that instant, fucked for eternity. Knowing at the same time that if it were possible to remain there forever, nothing would make sense. Not even pain, not even an orgasm. For a second the storm seemed joyful. Then the lightning made me very afraid.

In order not to feel inferior in the face of Ezequiel's scientific knowledge, I made a list for him of the different verbs in Spanish that describe an orgasm. In Cuba, for example, the say *venirse—to draw near*. I like that verb because it suggests moving toward someone. It is a verb for two. And essentially unisex. In Spain they say *correrse—to run*. Which implies almost the opposite. Taking off at the end, moving away from the other. It is a verb for men. In Argentina they say *acabar—to end*. It sounds like an order. Like a military exercise. A Peruvian woman friend calls it *llegar—to arrive*. Put like that, it sounds almost like utopia (and it often is). As though you were far away or needed more time. Her husband says *darla—to give it*. Curious. That sounds like an offering. Or, being pessimistic, like a favour done to you: here, take this. In which case it doesn't surprise me that my friend never *arrives*. In Guatemala they say *irse—to go*. A clear statement of abandonment. They need only add: *after you've paid*. In other countries they say *terminar—to finish*. Frustrating. It sounds like someone barges in and interrupts you halfway through. Here, though, perhaps because we are frontier people, we say *cruzar—to cross over*.

Are there places where they name women's orgasms? Where they say *I'm drowning, I'm dissolving, I'm unravelling, I'm irradiating*?

I asked Ezequiel which verb he liked best. He replied: That depends, Professor. When I'm on top, *venirme*. When I'm underneath, *llegar*. If I pick you up, *acabar*. From behind, *correrme*. When you blow me, *terminar*. When I'm outside you, *irme*. It depends.

Unable to sleep. At seven o'clock I gave up and got out of bed to see the sunrise. It felt like it rose too quickly. Everything happens more quickly than it ought to in summer.

I went out. It was hot. I waited for the shops to open. Standing in front of doors. Like an addict. I bought a lot of food for the day after tomorrow. Chicken, turkey, veal, low fat cheese (so as to feel less guilty), fruit yogurt (Lito hates the plain, sugar-free ones I eat), Coke (caffeine-free, of course, otherwise there is no getting the little angel to bed), good red wine, oranges, grapefruit, legumes for Mario (he needs lots of iron), vegetables for me, sweets for everyone. Then I found a see-through bra and knickers with suspenders. I'll wear that tonight.

$$\diamond \; \diamond \; \diamond$$

I call and call, but they don't answer. Every time this happens, I imagine Mario knows everything and is silently punishing me. Last night I dreamt he found Ezequiel hitchhiking on the motorway. He gave him a lift in the truck. And the two of them went off and left me on my own.

Lito doesn't reply to my messages. Mario doesn't call, and neither does Ezequiel. I have taken two aspirins and an anti-depressant. And have drunk two cups of strong coffee. I find it impossible to read. I feel horny. I think a lot about jumping out of the window. I want my husband and my son to come home now and not to come home. I want this house to return to normal and I will never be normal again. I don't want to see Ezequiel any more. I want to call Ezequiel and tell him to fuck me hard. I want him to hurt me. I want him to love me. I don't care what Ezequiel does. I would never fall in love with him. I hope he falls in love with me. I want to throw myself out of the window. I want to cause pain. Some of these things are true.

Work, work. That's all I know how to do. You have to be very sad to hate holidays. You are so responsible, people tell me. They can go to hell. I look for things to be responsible for because I can't be responsible for myself. Sometimes I think I don't deserve to be a mother. Sometimes I think I had a child in order to stop myself from jumping out of the window. Sometimes I think I should have been the one who got ill. Sometimes I think about being fucked hard. Women who know what they want never want anything interesting.

Hallelujah, they called, hallelujah. They are fine. Everything is fine. I am weeping. Lito is eating salads. Mario sounds normal. Nothing is awry. They are arriving tomorrow. So soon. Everything will go back to how it was. I'm going to leave the house spotless. I'm going to prepare a wonderful dinner for them. I'm going to read for a while. I'm going to text Ezequiel.

Message answered. Everything is as it should be. His place at ten. I like 10. It's a nice number. It looks like a whip taking aim at a backside. It's our last night. The night. The world is wonderful, terrible.

Mario

. . . a question only kids ask themselves for real, and then we sick people ask it again: is it okay to lie?, is it okay to be lied to?, a healthy grown-up won't even give it a thought, the answer seems obvious, right?, we learn to tell lies the same way we learn to talk, they teach us how to talk and then how to be quiet, I don't know, like when you play football, for example, first you kick the ball and then, unless you're stupid, you learn to not kick it, to move around tricking the other players, kids lie too, of course, I lied all the time when I was a kid, but, what I'm saying is, until you get to a certain age, you think it's wrong, that is the difference, I don't think we grown-ups are any worse, you know?, every kid contains the beginnings of a possible son of a bitch, this much I know, it's just that kids, and perhaps we adults are to blame for this, start by dividing the world into good and evil, truth and lies, the only time it's okay for them to lie is when they're playing, then it's allowed, so kids become grown-ups when they play, sort of the opposite of us parents, we play so we can be kids again, well, and then you grow up, and you lie and are lied to, and it isn't wrong, until one day, when you're sick, you begin to worry again about lies, you worry about them every time you talk to the doctors, your wife, your family, it's not a moral question, it's, I don't know, something physical, deep down you're scared stiff of the truth, but the idea of dying with a lie scares you even more, lies help us to carry on living, don't they?, and when you know you aren't going to carry on, you feel they're no use anymore, do you know what I mean?

Why am I talking about this?, ah, the weather thing, these painkillers make me half dopey, when you started doing the weather thing it made me laugh, you should have seen yourself, you were staring hard at the road, doing something with your finger on the windscreen, pulling faces, and soon after you told me the sky had changed, to begin with I played along because I thought it was a game, then, I'm not sure when, I started to realize you were serious, and besides you were so thrilled, from then on, I tell you, son, I spent the whole journey asking myself, do I tell him or not?, bah, best not, I thought, he'll find out for himself, but I don't know if you'd convinced yourself, or if it was a coincidence, or what, because you kept saying you'd guessed right, as a game I found it amusing, but as an expectation it was sad, if when you finally saw that the weather did as it pleased, that neither you nor I nor Pedro could do anything to change it, wouldn't you feel, I don't know, terribly small?, anyhow, maybe it's foolish and by now you don't even remember, but I didn't want to fall asleep today without telling you this.

From here, as soon as I open my eyes, I see the sky, as if I were in a plane, a very slow-moving plane, and you know what it looks like?, the dawn, I mean?, an insult, that's what it looks like to me, when I was young I was a night owl, I liked doing things while everyone was asleep, I felt untouchable, as you get older you become a lark, you start to worry about being late for things, night owls think they're stealing a march on everything, but the

moment they wake up they're already running late, since I got
sick I don't like the morning so much, it's, I don't know, too
loaded with expectations, and the silence of the night scares me,
I prefer the afternoon now, it's less demanding, so I'm watching
the sun go down, and I start to wonder, you see, where, where
the hell does beauty come from?, not from things, that's for sure,
I look at the tea tray, for instance, a grey plastic tray, slightly bat-
tered, with that curved edge things that are made to be stacked
have, covered in scratches from cutlery, the knife marks, one next
to the other, remind me of an electrocardiogram, the clusters of
dots from the forks, close up, are like dice pips, and suddenly this
tray turns into a thi—hold on, someone's knocking on the door.

At least this time they knocked, she must be a student nurse,
the older ones burst in, as if this were their room, recently I've
been eating more, I had lost a lot of weight, you saw me, I took
some appetite stimulants with me on the trip, they sort of worked,
it's hard to trust food when you keep throwing up, you start to
see it as something completely alien to your organism, I don't
know, some kind of invasive substance, I took the appetite stimulants and some other pills with me, none of them to cure me, all
to make me feel less, that's the weird thing about drugs, the ones
that supposedly cure you destroy you on the inside, and the ones
that supposedly aren't a cure make you feel like a person again,
does that mean you have to stop feeling like a person in order to
get better?, maybe that's why for so many of us it doesn't work, because we won't let the poison in completely.

The day of the race at the petrol station I'd been feeling sick
all day, I couldn't catch my breath, it happens sometimes, I don't
know what the hell it depends on, the heat, the humidity, being
tired, I've no idea, and you can run faster and faster, you train for
everything, bullheaded hare, it's like you had a pair of wheels in
your backside, you take after your granddad a little in that way,

he always used to say that it was fine to go down fighting, and, just to annoy him, I'd say: what about fighting to lose?, you were determined to beat me, weren't you, your legs are getting long, and you know the worst thing?, the most shameful thing?, when I saw you were pulling away from me I started to run for real, it upset me for a moment that you were going to win, then I realized I couldn't do it and I slowed down, I shut myself in the toilet, I waited in there for a while until I got my breath back, when I would insist on stopping for you to take a leak, for instance—no, it's nothing, hi, it's nothing.

Last night I watched a movie with your mum, she brought her laptop, good idea, a wonderful comedy with Katharine Hepburn, have you heard of her?, I mean, do people still know who Ms. Hepburn was?, the movie didn't seem dated, it's still hilarious and, how was it?, as wicked as intelligence itself, that's what your mother said last night, so don't give me the credit, I get distracted when I read, I think about a hundred and one other things, maybe that says something for books, I don't know, but it doesn't happen to me with movies, when I'm enjoying a movie, it's as though I disappear, if you follow me, at first I thought it was a bit frivolous of me, I mean, in my state, to laugh out loud like that, but I soon let myself go, and it worked better than any drug, it was a kind of, which reminds me, my pill.

Actually, well, there was another reason to enjoy the movie, being there, next to your mum, without talking, because what could we say to each other?, laughing at the same gags, the two of us just there, alive, knowing we love each other, and that we've hurt one another, that's the power of movies, right?, you are moved at the same time as others, you can share books as well, of course, that's what your mother always tells me, but we enjoy them separately, not together, maybe books are for people on their own,

I'm going to leave your mum on her own, whenever we both laughed she'd squeeze my hand.

Do you remember sometimes when she called us, there wasn't much coverage, we told her we'd call her at the next stop, and then we'd forget, and the poor woman kept calling, sick with worry, and I handed you the phone so she'd be less angry, sitting in the truck is like watching a really long movie, right?, your mum got upset, I think, she ended up not always answering her phone, I could tell she was tense, I kept saying we were fine, I don't know whether she believed me, I had a few dizzy spells, the worst one was on the way there, in Tucumancha, I was even scared I'd let go of the wheel, the road was full of bends, I hadn't driven that much in years, it was early on in the journey, and I was still telling myself: I can do it, I can do it, I must be able to do it, like you with the weather, right?, we're both bullheaded, you and I, dizzier and dizzier, and there was nowhere to stop on that stretch of road, and that's when I got really worried, that's when I thought your mother was right and the trip had been a crazy idea, and I remembered Uncle Juanjo, who'd suggested I get some practice before setting off, and I remembered your granddad, who did exercises every morning for half an hour, and all of a sudden I thought I was an irresponsible father, I think this was what made me feel the dizziest.

And what about the fan?, the one you said was going to unscrew itself from the ceiling and slice our heads off?, we stopped there because I was lost, son, what a disaster, I turned back three or four times, I couldn't even understand the instructions on the GPS, the roads weren't right, they'd changed, I didn't feel good that day either, it's strange, for the most part I felt worse on the way there than on the way back, that night what I needed was a comfortable bed, bah, a bed in any case, what a crappy mattress, right?, but what I think about most now, what I most remember, is when we slept next to each other in the truck, on our sides, pretty uncomfortably, and I clasped your chest, I could feel you breathe and I didn't sleep a wink, I stayed awake all night, euphoric, listening to every sound . . .

Lito

All the houses in Comala de la Vega are low and the aerials are crooked. I bet whenever it's windy the TVs change channel. Dad said we had to stop. I didn't want to take a leak. I think this changed the weather a bit. It looked like rain. And in the end there wasn't a single drop.

Dad has invented a game. Each time we come to a town I have to guess how many people live there. If I get it more or less right I'm allowed to order another dessert instead of a salad. The day before yesterday I got two towns right and three wrong. Yesterday I got four right and two wrong. So far today is a draw at two all. I don't think anybody lives in Comala de la Vega. The streets are empty. The only thing moving is Pedro. All the cars look really old. Like they've been there for a thousand years. If the traffic lights went off nothing would happen. Who turns the traffic lights on and off? I have to ask Dad, who has just called Mum. I don't like the way he gets all serious when he talks to her. I'm worried they're talking about me. We leave Pedro under some trees so he doesn't get hot. Dad's still on the phone. The only thing he says is yes yes, no no, I know I know.

We go into a café called La Plata. Amazing. There's someone in there. Three people. A lady sweeping the floor. A man selling lottery tickets. And the waiter. Dad orders two coffees with milk and goes to the toilet. I follow him. There are a ton of smells in the toilet. The walls have got writing all over them. Most of the words I don't even understand. They'd fail handwriting at my school. One sentence says: Live and let die. It doesn't make sense. There are also drawings of willies and boobs. They do make sense. Big willies and round boobs. Suddenly I hear noises coming from the other cubicles. I don't know if it's someone groaning or the pipes. I stay quiet for a bit. Nothing. I call out to Dad. There's no answer. I'm not afraid or anything. But just in case I run out. Without washing my hands.

Dad is talking to the waiter. When they see me come out they go quiet. I take a sip of coffee. It tastes like mud. The lady sweeping the floor goes past and says to me: Ah, what a cute young man. Dad says: You're so right, señora. The lottery guy asks: Sure you don't want a ticket, sir? Dad says: I'd lose. The man says: You never know, sir. Dad asks: How much do I owe you, boss? The lady answers: The young man's is on the house. Dad looks at me: Aren't you going to say thank you, Lito? I say: Thanks a lot, señora. The lady shouts: Ah, what a little angel. I leave half my coffee.

By the café's door there's a showcase full of watches. Big ones. Gold. With hands. And the day of the week and the date. And a special button for the light. They're all Lewis Valentinos. They have to be good. I stay looking at the watches. I've never had one. Of course I was only nine before. Suddenly Dad's arm appears. We go outside. It's a bit cooler now. Dad, I say, what kind of watch do you have? I don't wear one anymore, son, he tells me. Yes, I say, but when you did. I don't remember, he says, your mother always gave them to me as presents. And did you ever have a Lewis Valentino? I insist. I don't know that brand, he says, messing up my fringe. They're awesome, I explain.

Dad gives me a stick of gum. Raspberry flavoured. I chew it really slowly. With my back teeth. So all the juice comes out. I bought them at the café, says Dad, they had other ones that (on the hillsides I can see a, what do you call it? a herd? a flock? of wind turbines. Over there. So tall. So silent. Actually I don't know if they're silent, because they're miles away. Wind turbines are always miles away. Maybe because actually they're really noisy. Like aeroplane propellers. I bet if they were pulled out of the ground they'd float. Or do you need two propellers to float?, is that why planes always have two wings?, or are there planes with only one wing? I imagine the wind turbines taking off from the hills and bits dropping off them, like those little white plants when you blow on them, they), huh, Lito, do you want it or not? What? I say, as I stop looking out of the window. The packet, son, the packet, Dad sighs. Oh, thanks, I tell him. I love raspberry gum. Hey, I say, I know how many people live in Comala de la Vega. Go on? Dad says. Three, I tell him. He smiles. Then he looks at the map and writes something down. Well, Dad says, I think we're going to get there a bit late tonight.

There's no gum left. I don't get Dad. Sometimes when I'm not hungry we stop to eat. Other times my stomach makes louder noises than Pedro's engine and we just keep going. Gum always cheats you. Just when you're happily chewing, it runs out. All you're left with is a lump of plastic in your mouth. An eraser. A journey is the opposite of a stick of gum. At first you don't expect anything. And you always find something.

Mum writes on Dad's phone:

How are things with you, treasure? Are you happy?
Mum made a chocolate cake while you were away,

```
I'm practising for when you get back! Is your
Daddy driving a lot? Please make sure he rests. I
love you, darling.
```

I reply:

```
Hi M Im fine all dy on rd hpe Pdro rsts @ nite!
do u no wot brnd D's wtchs wre pls kp me choc mch
xxx msu
```

Dad looks at me out of the corner of his eye while I text. Why don't you call her instead? he asks, she prefers to hear your voice. I know, I explain, but the battery's low. And I haven't played golf yet. Golf? Dad says. America or Europe? I ask. What? he says, surprised. Just tell me which you prefer, I insist, America or Europe? Oh, Lito, Dad answers, how should I know? Europe? Okay, Europe, I say selecting the championship.

In Región there's this weird wind blowing. It goes then comes back. Like a boomerang. It pushes you from behind. Goes on for a few yards. Then it blows dust in your face. Is the wind here always like this? I ask, rubbing my eyes. Always, Dad answers, except when it takes an afternoon nap. I can see the wind pushes Dad even harder from the front. He walks slowly taking small steps. We cross the road to the opposite building. There's a fat guy with a shaven head in the doorway. He's wearing shades though it's already dark. He's dressed in a black suit, a striped T-shirt and sandals. He has huge arms and a really small head. Dad whispers in his ear. He puts something in his jacket pocket. The fat guy nods his head slightly. I bet if he nods any harder, it'll roll off like a bowling ball.

A girl with a shell necklace and green lipstick greets us. No. It can't be green. Or can it? The lights are fluorescent! The girl sees me hiding behind Dad and smiles. She has blue teeth. In reception there are mirrors broken on purpose. And plastic flowers in ice-cream glasses. The girl asks us not to open the blinds in the room because they're stuck. Besides, she winks, with this wind it's best you don't even try. After she winks, her top eyelashes come off and get tangled in her bottom eyelashes. I want to tell her but I'm too shy. Dad whispers in my ear: Gorilla from Manila, there's good news and bad. The good news is they have Internet. The bad news is it isn't working.

We go upstairs to put our things in our room. The carpet smells of cigarettes. It has holes bigger than my feet. You could play mini-golf on it. Lito, Dad says, looking at the carpet, whatever you do, don't walk around barefoot. And when you go to bed, take the quilt off first, do you hear? I spot two white towels on a chair. Well, more or less white. I sniff them. Luckily they smell of soap. I open the bathroom door. There are only wire hangers and a safe. What a weird room. Dad goes into the hallway. I hear him talking to himself. This is impossible! he mutters, I told that bitch we wanted en suite! The word *bitch* always makes me giggle. I like it when Dad says it. It doesn't sound the same when my friends and I say it. Dad comes back in. He picks up the towels. He says to me: At least there's hot water in the shower. Bring your clothes, son. And please do as I say, and don't touch anything, okay?

In the bar I gobble down two cheeseburgers. A plate of chips with tons of hot sauce. And a scoop of ice cream covered in syrup. Dad only eats half his. He says he wants to lose some more weight. He takes an aspirin with a glass of water. Before he got the virus he used to eat loads. And he loved going to restaurants. What? I laugh, my mouth full of ice cream, so you didn't like your big fat belly? What about you, skinny chops? he teases, are you sure you don't need another hamburger? I don't know what time it is. I would if I had a Lewis Valentino. I don't feel like going to bed yet. Travelling is tiring but it wakes me up.

Dad leaves the table. He goes over to the bar. He pays. He is looking at me. Very hard. I think that as soon as I finish my ice cream we're going to have to go up to the room. Oof. Dad is coming back. He walks up to me. He lifts my head in his hands. And he suggests we stay and have a drink. A drink! Dad and me! In a bar! After dark! I can't believe it. It's totally awesome. I get up. I wipe the syrup off my mouth with my sleeve. I stand up very straight. And we walk together to the bar. Dad orders a whisky. I order a Fanta. With lots and lots of ice.

People start arriving. The music is louder. The girl with the green lips begins serving drinks. I look at her eyelashes. She's fixed them. I wave to her. She pretends not to see me. Even though I'm sitting on a high stool. I clink glasses with Dad. The ice cubes wobble and get smaller. I remember the lifeboats in *Titanic*. Leonardo DiCaprio freezing to death in the sea with Kate somebody or other. Wil? Wing? Somebody touches my arm.

I turn round. It's a man in a baseball cap. He looks at Dad. He points outside and says: A good truck, huh boss? Dad nods. Nothing beats a Peterbilt, huh, boss? says the man in the cap. Dad finishes his drink. Are you a trucker? I ask. No, dear boy, the man in the cap smiles, I'm a magician. Really? I say surprised, you do magic tricks? Not tricks, he says, I make reality, magic is real. But do you do magic tricks or not? I insist. Of course, he says, of course. Suddenly Dad looks like he's in a bad mood. I'm thrilled. I've always wanted to know how to do magic tricks. If they are tricks, that is. Let's see, I say, how do rabbits appear? Rabbits, the magician answers, appear on their own. They don't need any help. It's Mother Nature, you get it? And what about people, I ask, how do they get sawed in half? Ah, says the magician, taking a sip of his drink, that's even more interesting. Only people who want to get sawed in half get cut in half. The others don't. The others use tricks. And how does the trick work? I ask impatiently. Look, look, the magician says, very serious. He picks up a napkin. He folds it in two. He shows it to me. Then he folds it in two again. And he shows it to me again. You see? he says. I look at the napkin. This napkin is many napkins at once. It's one. Two. Four. It's the same with people. Dad says: Come along, son, it's late. Wait, wait, I say, he's explaining a trick to me. Son, it's late, insists Dad. The magician looks him in the eye and says: Calm down, calm down. He looks like he's going to hypnotize him. Dad leaves a banknote on the bar. He takes my hand and leaves without waiting for the change. Boss, the magician calls out. Dad keeps walking. We're not being polite. One moment, boss, the magician says again. Dad slows down and squeezes my hand hard. I've got a present for Lito, the magician says, guessing my name. Don't trouble yourself, Dad answers for me. I insist, says the magician. And he takes off his cap. And I put it on. The lights bounce off his forehead. Like a Christmas tree. This cap, he explains, transforms you. It's yours. Don't forget that.

Before turning off the light, I put the magic cap on again. For God's sake take that thing off, Dad says from his bed, don't be stupid. I need to know if it's true, I say. That guy, he complains, was crazy. We'll see, I answer, turning off the light.

We wake up late. The first thing I do as soon as I get up is look in the mirror. Very closely. I don't notice anything. I put the cap in my backpack. Dad gives me a kiss. We get dressed quickly. We wash our faces in the hallway. We go down to breakfast. The magician is sitting at one of the tables. He nods at us. He has bags under his eyes. Maybe he never sleeps. I go over to him and say: I'm the same, you see? The magician looks me up and down and answers: No. You're not the same. You'll soon see.

We drive the first few miles in silence. Dad, I say suddenly, do I look different to you? Of course! he answers, you've changed into a raccoon golfer.

Elena

It's morning again. Nothing begins.

Impossible to sleep. Perhaps because Mario and Lito are finally home. Or from mixing pills. Or because yesterday I told Ezequiel that I'm not going to see him any more.

As I write, Mario is snoring louder than ever. As though, by breathing in, he's trying to find all the strength he has lost. This racket doesn't bother me today. It tells me he is alive.

He has shadows under his eyes, drawn features, no belly. There is a paleness about him that doesn't seem to come from a lack of sunshine, but from somewhere deeper. A sort of white glow beneath the skin. There, between his ribs.

When Mario opened the door, I was shocked. I'm not sure whether he had really come back so diminished, or whether I had been expecting the robust figure who only exists in my memory now. He seemed in good spirits. He smiled as before. He had the look of a mission accomplished. As soon as I kissed him I felt like crying, running away. I had to switch quickly to Lito, hug him very tight, focus on his soft cheeks, his supple hands, and his agile body, in order to regain some composure.

Because they were late and I was becoming increasingly anxious, I had been unable to stifle the urge to call Ezequiel. It was then, almost at the end of the conversation, that I told him it was impossible to go on. That being alone these past weeks had deranged me. And that now I had to go back to my normal routine and my family duties. He agreed with everything I said. He told me he expected no less of me. That my decision was the right one. That he understood, really he did. And then, without altering the tone of his voice, he started describing what he would do to me when I next went to his house. I became incensed. He laughed and went on talking filth to me, and I started insulting him, and the rage of my insults turned into a desire to hit him, humiliate him, mount him. He started groaning into the mouthpiece, and I began to touch myself. Then I heard the sounds of the lock.

While I was heating up the dinner, I studied the inside of the oven and thought of Sylvia Plath. I uncorked the wine. I lit some candles. During the meal, I started to feel better. Lito kept telling me stories about their trip, he was so excited. Mario nodded, with a gleam in his eyes. If the evening had ended at that precise moment, if, let's say, the ceiling had suddenly caved in on me, I would have closed my eyes believing I was happy.

Before dessert the three of us made a toast, laughing like any normal family, and Mario poured half a glass of wine for Lito. I couldn't help wondering if he had done the same during the trip. I didn't dare ask. We drank. We joked. We enjoyed our dessert. We put Lito to bed. The two of us sat down together. We held hands. And we stayed up talking until a glimmer began filtering through the curtains. Then all of a sudden Mario seemed to shut down.

Now he is snoring. I am watching him.

I fan him, feed him, bathe him, listen to him, try to guess what he is feeling. And I don't know, I don't know what else to do.

These blasts of pain throughout his body. They have no precise location, they meander. I go mad trying to discover where it hurts. As though his affliction were another skin.

He no longer leaves the house. Lito asks what's the matter with him. I explain that Dad is exhausted after the trip and has a bad case of the flu. I'm not sure he believes me. He looks thoughtful. Occasionally he talks to me about a cap.

The pills aren't enough. For him or for me.

My brothers-in-law arrive tomorrow. They give their opinions a lot, especially over the phone. But they are less keen on coming here and looking Mario in the eye. They barely touch their brother when they visit him. As if his body were radioactive.

Lito will be thrilled. He loves his uncles. He and Juanjo talk about cars and watch action movies. Those Stallone horrors. Juanjo's taste in movies is rather peculiar. Stallone's only noteworthy performance was in a porn movie, I seem to recall. Lito and his youngest uncle shut themselves in his room and listen to music online. My son is twenty years his junior, yet they have the same mental age. He sees much less of his other uncle, who has hundreds of children and dresses them all identically.

Of course Mario is happy about their visit, too. But happiness in him has become muddied. You need to dig down to see it. All of a sudden it appears, from beneath his hostile looks.

Juanjo is going to stay for a few days. And nights.

I make beds, make infusions, make food, make assumptions. Whenever I am on my own, I turn my phone off.

Mario's brothers are coming in a few hours. And so is all the rest. What's coming is That. Everything is descending on me. From time to time I leave the bedroom to take a cold shower.

I've just turned my phone on.

I couldn't. Resist.

Full stop. Pointless to justify myself.

He was understanding. He let me hit him. Then we talked about movies.

He penetrated me only at the very end, all at once. It was like being healed.

I got hold of a colleague who asked no questions. She agreed to ring me at home at a prearranged time and, following my instructions, asked to speak to me. Pretending I was busy with something else, I let my brothers-in-law pick up the phone. The moment they passed me the receiver, my colleague hung up as agreed. I carried on talking to myself and concocted a meeting at her place to prepare the school exams. I was surprised by her willingness. I thought she was more prudish. She has three children.

That's what we talked about, movies. Ezequiel doesn't like classic movies at all. He makes fun of my taste, thinks they are pedantic. He says I consider any old nonsense in black and white a gem or the predecessor of something. He says today's movies can't hide behind these excuses. They are either good or bad. Full stop. I have started using that stupid expression of his, *full stop*. That's his approach to life. And to movies. If the characters suffer, he's interested. If they have fun, he's bored.

Ezequiel told me he had just seen a film starring Kate Winslet. He's crazy about Kate Winslet. He says she's as beautiful as a plain woman can be, or as thin as a fat woman can be. Winslet's lover is a premature ejaculator (in other words, he's a man) and after a fuck, she reproaches him: It's not about you! Ezequiel explained that at the beginning he thought this was a good expression. But that later he had realized it was a lie. A piece of pseudofeminist demagoguery, he said. I was immediately on my guard, tried to gainsay him, but he continued undaunted. He said the premature ejaculator's problem is the exact opposite. The poor guy is incapable of feeling any pleasure. He has no idea how to get any. He has to begin by enhancing his own pleasure. Making it more complex. Only in this way can men pleasure women as well. "We have to be good in bed out of pure selfishness. A useful selfishness." That is what he told me. "And then the others thank you. The same as in medicine."

He rarely gets out of bed, he feels sick, and when he does get out of bed he feels worse. It's as if he is walking along the top of a wall. His voice quavers. It doesn't matter how much he eats, he continues losing weight. His muscles, his bones, his veins ache. We can't keep up the deception that this is the flu. He still goes on pretending. Every time Lito goes near him he grins like a dummy, takes out the thermometer, cracks jokes that make me want to weep. I sometimes think that deceiving his son brings him a measure of relief. Within these fictions, he is still not critically ill.

I change sheets, cook, keep quiet. I come and go like a sleep-walker. I think things I don't want to think.

I have just left Lito at my parents' house. He is going to stay with them until school starts. I prefer to spare him this memory. If they take him to the beach house, even better. Childhood always seemed easy there. My sister says she is looking for flights.

Juanjo came to look after Mario. Each time I explained some detail about his brother's care, he gave me a look as if to say he already knew. Juanjo likes to have the last word. Not by winning the argument, but by being emphatic. He needs to impose his personality rather than his opinion. This is precisely why he is an easy man to please. He seems very obliging of late. I have the impression that, all of a sudden, he has recognized himself in his older brother. As if he could sense the danger to himself.

When it was time to leave, Mario appeared, impeccably dressed. He had even polished his shoes. He looked serious and had difficulty moving, concentrating on every step. He went down to the garage with us. I ran to the car so Lito wouldn't see my face. Through the rearview mirror, I watched Mario bend over to embrace him and rest his head on his shoulder. It looked like he was playing an instrument.

My parents say Lito is fine. My parents say they are fine. My parents have always believed that things are less frightening when they are fine. Not me. When things are going fine, I think they are about to get worse and I feel even more scared.

When I spoke to Dad, he said almost exactly what Mum

had said to me. It is astounding that they still understand each other after a lifetime of marriage. They both offered, independently, to come and stay at the house. I told each of them no, that I prefer them to look after Lito, to shield him from this. Mum insisted I shouldn't try to carry the whole burden on my own. Dad advised me not to try to appear stronger than I am, because it will only harm me more. Sometimes I can't stand having such understanding parents. Not being able to criticize them frustrates me. They raised me in an atmosphere of tolerance, respect, and communication. In other words, they left me alone with my traumas. As though, each time I look for someone to point the finger at, they responded from inside my head: We aren't to blame.

Lito told me his granddad still plays football. He sounded surprised. He doesn't run very much, he gets tired, but he has a good aim and he can kick the ball with both feet. Granddad isn't that old, he said.

There was no other choice.

I debated. I debated for weeks. Day and night.

There is no other choice, no other anything. He needs help. I need help.

But not the sort that came. Because he did come.

He turned up quite naturally. I had implored him to advise me over the phone. But he insisted on seeing Mario in person. He said it was his duty and this was his patient. And he announced a time. And he hung up. And, right on time, the bell rang.

When I opened the door to him, I felt a sort of whirling sensation. We hadn't seen each other since my brothers-in-law had visited. I looked him up and down. In his tailor-made suit.

His hair was slightly damp. Ezequiel greeted me as though we scarcely knew one another. He pronounced my name in a neutral voice. He proffered his hand. His hand. And he went up to the bedroom. The bedroom.

He sat down beside Mario. He asked him a few questions. He helped him unbutton his pyjama top. He examined him carefully. He ran a stethoscope over his chest. He took his pulse, his blood pressure, his temperature. Mario seemed to trust him blindly. The tact with which he treated him, the concern with which he spoke to him, the sensitivity with which he touched him was admirable. Despicable. Ezequiel whispered, Mario nodded. I watched them from the bedroom doorway. Neither of them said a word to me.

And something else. Something that places me on a level with rats. Self-aware rats, at least. While I watched Ezequiel touching my husband in our bed, sliding his hands over Mario's shoulders, his shoulder bones, his stomach, I suddenly felt jealous. Of the two of them.

When the examination was over, Ezequiel spoke to me alone. He described Mario's condition to me soberly, in the voice of Dr. Escalante. He increased the dosage of one drug. He took him off another. He made a couple of practical suggestions. And he expressed his opinion about admitting him to a hospital. And he was right. And I told him he was right. And he walked down the stairs. And he proffered his hand once more. And he left my house.

Me. The rodent.

So this was how it was. This was it. Being there.

I'm surprised how quickly, in a place destined to break all our habits, we establish new routines. We aren't creatures of habit:

the creature is habit itself. It sinks its teeth into its quarry and won't let go.

I spend all my nights there. I try to see that Mario gets some rest. I give him water. I tuck him in. I ensure his chest goes up and down. I listen to him breathe. When he falls asleep, I read with a torch. I am afraid to switch it off. It feels like something will end.

After lunch I go home, and return to the hospital at dinner-time. Mario prefers to be left alone in the afternoons. He was insistent about this. He brooks no dissent. He finds arguing increasingly unbearable. Sometimes he lets his gaze wander, float. He looks at something that is apparently in his lap. A sort of miniature world we others can't see.

When I go into the room, dressed in the clothes he likes, my hair styled for him, I can sense resentment in his eyes. As though my liveliness offended him. How are you, my love? I said to him this morning. Here I am, dying, and you? he grumbled. Yesterday he had replied: Eating shit, thank you very much. He refuses to let them increase the morphine. He says he prefers to be awake, he wants to be aware.

Try as I might, I can't look at Mario with the same eyes, either. Suddenly his every act, every trivial gesture like yawning, smiling, or biting into a piece of toast, seems to belong to a remote language. His silences make me anxious, now. I listen to them intently, I try to interpret them. And I am never sure what they are saying. I think of what they will say to me when this is all I have, a background silence.

Pity has its own way of destroying. It's a noise that disturbs everything Mario says or doesn't say to me. At night, by his bedside, the noise prevents me from sleeping. When the light goes out, a sort of glow surrounds, or perhaps encroaches on everything Mario has done. The past is already being manipulated by the future. It is a dizzying capsize. An intimate science fiction.

Last night I took with me to the hospital an essay Virginia Woolf wrote about her own illness. I was curious to know whether this text would guide me or drag me down further. Yet I sensed I was going to find something there. Something in the language Mario now speaks. I fell asleep almost at the end. When I woke up I wasn't sure I had actually read it. Until I saw what I'd underlined. With nothing to lean on and my unsteady hand, they looked like crossings-out.

"We cease to be soldiers in the army of the upright; we become deserters," that is the ambivalence of the sick, which explains why I sometimes feel angry with him. He has been shot down, yes, he has been shot in the back. But because of this he has left us. As though he had abandoned us to join a war no one else knows about.

"To hinder the description of illness in literature, there is the poverty of the language. English, which can express the thoughts of Hamlet and the tragedy of Lear," or Alonso Quijano, De Pablos, Funes, "has no words for the shiver and the headache. It has all grown one way. The merest schoolgirl, when she falls in love, has Shakespeare or Keats to speak her mind for her," or Garcilaso, Bécquer, Neruda, "but let a sufferer try to describe a pain in his head to a doctor and language at once runs dry," hence this desperate need of words?

"What ancient and obdurate oaks are uprooted in us by the act of sickness," and these great trunks topple for both the sick and their carers, both endure a second operation that amputates something akin to their roots. "When we think of this, as we are so frequently forced to think of it, it becomes strange indeed that illness has not taken its place with love and battle and jealousy among the prime themes of literature," or perhaps it isn't so strange: Who wants to make a fire from the wood of their own tree?

Since Mario has been sleeping at the hospital, I have to be on standby during the night. My nerves are electrified from not taking tranquillizers. One day my head will shut down all of a sudden, like when a fuse blows. Delayed sleep is degenerating into a habit. Into a sort of insomniac workout. My normal state is this mixture of lack of rest and inability to rest. And so I write.

Sometimes I find myself watching the other patients and their relatives, and I have trouble telling them apart. Not because they look alike (health is so painfully obvious that it makes you ashamed in front of the sick), but because, deep down, we are all doing the same thing: trying to salvage what we have left.

By caring for our sick person, we are protecting their present. A present in the name of a past. What am I protecting of myself? This is where the future comes in (or hurls itself out of the window). For Mario it is inconceivable. He can't even speculate about it. The future: not its prediction but the simple possibility of it. In other words, its true liberty. That is what the illness kills off before killing off the sick.

This unknown time, this section of me, is what I am perhaps trying to salvage. So that everything that has been done wrong, not done, half done, won't crush me tomorrow. For us carers, the future widens like an all-engulfing crater. In the centre there is already someone missing. Illness as a meteorite.

What is to be done? Action seems terribly obvious: to care for, to watch over, to keep warm, to feed. But what about my imagination, which has also become ill? Is it wrong of me to plan ahead, to rehearse again and again what is to come? Am I preparing myself for the loss of Mario? Or am I snatching away what little I have left of him?

I mentioned this to Ezequiel once, a while ago, when he was only Dr. Escalante. We were in his office. Mario had gone to the toilet. I took the opportunity to ask him about the appropriateness of planning ahead. I remember Ezequiel saying to me: If you don't live in the present today, tomorrow you won't know how to live in the future. I found his Zen-like tone rather irritating. I asked him to be more specific. But Mario came back from the toilet. And Ezequiel smiled and didn't say anything anymore.

I keep coming across books that are appropriate for hospitals. I don't mean books that distract me (it's impossible to be distracted in a hospital), but rather that help me understand why the hell we are there. Where I am not convinced we should be. Where I brought him to leave him in other people's hands. Now, when I read, I search for him. The books speak to me more than he and I speak to one another. I read about the sick and the dead and widows and orphans. The sum of all the stories could fit into this list.

"Then he took out a syringe," I underlined last night in a short story by Flannery O'Connor, "and prepared to find the vein, humming a hymn as he pressed the needle in." When they inject

Mario I find it impossible to watch; they usually talk to him about something else while they are doing it, and I have the impression that what they say reaches his vein too. "He lay with a rigid outraged stare while the privacy of his blood was invaded by this idiot," Mario says that what he most hates about being in a hospital is that as he gets worse, everyone feels obliged to put on a hopeful face for him. "He gazed down into the crater of death," the crater!, "and fell back dizzy on his pillow," every so often, Mario cranes his neck, lifts his head, and lets it drop again.

Every night, between paragraphs, I watch Mario sleep and I wonder what he is dreaming about. Does one dream differently in a hospital bed? Because, to be sure, one reads very differently.

Cold, always cold, he feels cold in summer; even though they cover him, he shivers. It is as if his skin no longer warmed him.

Heat can be an extreme sensation, but it doesn't accuse anyone. If one person is suffering from it, the other doesn't feel at fault. When Mario grows cold, on the other hand, I feel I am letting him down. That I should keep him warm but don't know how. I ask the nurses if they couldn't perhaps turn the heating on, and they look at me pityingly.

I find it hard to leave. In the hospital I sustain my mission. My mission sustains me. Life outside is becoming more difficult. I don't know whether there is a name for this abduction. Fleming's Syndrome? When I don't look after anyone, no one looks after me.

Every afternoon, when I open the front door and hang my bag on the coat stand, I realize how big this house is going to be. I walk through its emptiness. It seems to have been furnished by strangers. Not only is my husband missing, and my son, whom I call obsessively. I, too, am missing here. Although the objects appear intact, time has spread itself over them. Like a museum of our own lives. I am the only visitor and also an intruder.

There is no one here. No one in me. The person who cries, eats, has a nap, goes to the bathroom, is someone else. I hesitate to see my friends because they always ask the same questions. I don't evade them either, because I am afraid they will stop asking. When I go to bed, as I close my eyes, I have fantasies about not waking up. As soon as I open them, the ceiling caves in on me.

I need some aggression. I need somebody to remind me I exist in myself. I need Ezequiel like a line. Like a gram, a kilo, a whole body. I am not talking about love. Love can't enter when there's no one home. Or if it does, it finds nothing. I am talking about urgent assistance. Emergency resuscitation. I want to be humiliated to the point where I no longer care. I want to be a virgin, not to have felt anything.

I switch on the radio. I don't listen to the voices. I turn on the television. I don't watch the pictures. I go from YouTube to my bank, from Facebook to books, from politics to porn. The wheel on the mouse is reminiscent of the clitoris. The fingertip controls forgetting. I browse the headlines, I contemplate the catastrophe of the world through a glass, I slide over its surface. I try to absorb the absence of pain because I am not the one suffering in other places, in other news. Does this offer me any relief? Yes. No. Yes.

In the inertia of my searches to discover what it is I am searching for, almost without realizing I tap in: help.

The first result is "psychological help." Online therapy.

The second result is the Wikipedia entry that defines and classifies the word *help*.

The third result is help in configuring broadband settings.

The fourth result directs me to the Twitter help centre: "Getting started," "Troubles," and "Report violations." It sounds like the sequence of an attack.

The fifth result helps with editing content. Assuming the user has any.

The sixth result is from the search engine itself: help with searching.

I am not surfing. But sinking.

"In the past," I underline in a novel by Kenzaburo Ōe, "a siren had always been a moving object: it appeared in the distance, sped by, moved away", disappearing completely, while I gave, at most, a fleeting consideration to the imagined sufferer and then forgot about it, as you forget a sound you no longer hear. "But now, I wore a siren stuck to my body like an illness", the illness rotating on itself, my back transporting it. "This siren was never going to recede". Every time I hear an ambulance, I am afraid it is coming for us.

In a while, I'll return to the hospital. I only had time to go home, take a shower, and change my clothes. I didn't have a nap this afternoon.

He always accepts. But he never takes the initiative of calling me. His only initiatives with me (and he seems to reserve them, to savagely preserve them) take place in bed. I asked him whether this is part of the protocol, or what. Ezequiel simply replied: This is in your hands.

Each time I go to bed with him, I feel disloyal not only because of Mario. Also because of Lito. I have the feeling I am neglecting him, abandoning him, when Ezequiel penetrates me. As though, when he does it, he reminds me I am a mother. Then I feel the urge to tell him to penetrate me harder, deeper, in order to give me back my son. I have monstrous orgasms. They hurt bad. He thinks this is good. He finds it healthy.

The more I see Ezequiel, the guiltier I feel. And the guiltier I feel, the more I tell myself that I deserve some satisfaction too. That from time immemorial heads of families have enjoyed their mistresses, while their foolish wives were dutifully faithful. And the more I push myself to escape with Ezequiel. Although I realize that in the end I am not escaping anything.

Every day, at some point, the room doors close in the hospital. All of them. At once. Then a metal gurney goes down the corridor. A gurney draped in sheets.

I look out and see these gurneys go by with a mixture of horror and relief. I watch the nursing assistants pushing them, I hear the wheels turning. Every day they take someone. Every day they bring a replacement. This stream of bodies isolates our room, where we are still safe. This stream also tells me that, at some point, someone will stick their head out of another ward and see me walking behind a gurney. And they will have the same pointless reprieve I have now.

Knowing what will happen, how and where, every gesture contains an element of deception. I bring him newspapers, films, sweets. We call Lito, we chat with Mario's brothers, we speak of happy memories. I smile at him, I caress him, I make jokes. I feel as if I were part of a conspiracy. As if we all were forcing a dying man to pretend he isn't dying.

I have the impression that families, and doctors, too, perhaps, soothe the sick in order to protect themselves from their agony. As a buffer against the excessive, unbearable disorder which the ugliness of another's death creates in the midst of one's own life.

"Writing about illness," I underlined last night in an essay by Roberto Bolaño, "especially if one is seriously ill oneself, can be an ordeal. But it is also a liberating act," I hope this applies to us carers too, "exercising the tyranny of illness," this is something we never talk about, and it is true: the oppressed need to oppress, the threatened want to threaten, the sick yearn to disrupt the health of others, "it is a diabolical temptation," we carers also have temptations, especially of the diabolical variety.

"What did Mallarmé mean when he said the flesh was sad and that he had read all the books? That he was sated with reading and sated with fucking? That, beyond a certain moment, every book and every act of carnal knowledge is a repetition?" I very much doubt it, that moment could only be marriage, "I believe Mallarmé is speaking of illness, of the battle it unleashes against health, two totalitarian states or powers," illness not only takes control of everything, it also rereads everything, makes things speak to us of it. "The image that Mallarmé constructs speaks of illness as a resignation to living. And to turn around this defeat he unsuccessfully opposes reading and sex." What else could we oppose?

The two of us lie on our backs in his bed, shoulder to shoulder, covered in sweat, catching our breath, floating in that fleeting moment of oblivion. I tried to go from my body to the idea. I think better after I have felt my entire body.

I asked him whether, beyond genetics, he believed psychological factors were at work in illnesses such as Mario's. According to some theories, Ezequiel replied, we become ill in order to find out whether we are loved.

I dressed and slammed the door.

I called my mother in tears. She told me I was right to get it off my chest. Immediately, as if through telepathy, my sister called me. She asked me how Mario was and told me about some flights she had just found.

When I contemplate him, skinny and white as any sheet, I sometimes think: This isn't Mario. It can't be him. My Mario was different, not like this at all.

Yet at other times I wonder: What if this is the real Mario? And rather than having lost his essence, what remains is the essential part of him? Like a distillation? What if we are misinterpreting our loved ones' bodies?

I have just said goodbye to Ezequiel from the door of our house, as if this were the most natural thing in the world, as if we had no neighbours, after talking to him, arguing with him, having two sessions in bed with him, in our marriage bed.

It all started with a coffee. I sent him a text message and he replied instantly. He was thinking about me a lot today. And I needed a bit of company, he said. And he wasn't far from my place. And we could at least have a coffee. And, and.

I think he came here with this in mind. The idea of going this far excited him. Well: there it is. There is nothing more for us to defile.

For God's sake. *He* came here with this in mind?

I'm going to take a couple of pills. It's not as if there is much in me that can be fixed.

"In bed, at night," I underlined in a Justo Navarro novel, "I was crushed by the horror of things being exactly the same as when I was alive although I wasn't," I know Mario is scared to death of dying in his sleep, which is why he doesn't sleep, "and so I counted my teeth with the tip of my tongue to rid myself of the fear of being dead, and I fell asleep counting my teeth. And I woke up: the fear was greater right before opening my eyes," every night I try to make him fall asleep and I am alarmed every time he does, I do my best to make him rest and then pray silently this won't be his final rest. Some waiting is like a slow death. It is stifling waiting for a death in order to start my own life again, knowing full well that, when it happens, I will be incapable of doing so.

Last night I dreamt Ezequiel was examining my husband, he could hear something in his skin, he performed an emergency operation and extracted tiny foetuses from him.

Mario

. . . like we were having a coffee together the day after tomorrow, right?, I rest for a while after lunch, and as soon as I open my eyes the words come to me, sometimes I even dream what I'm going to say to you, and then, when I say it, I feel like I'm repeating myself, actually we wouldn't be able to have a decent cup of coffee here, okay, so they give you some black, or dark brown stuff, a sort of baby poo, thank God your mum gets it from the machine downstairs, she always rushes back up, poor thing, so it doesn't go cold, how about a green tea?, the nurses sometimes ask me, you don't want a green tea?, listen, I tell them, do you think this calls for tea?

What was the name of that café in Comala de la Vega?, La . . . ?, what was it called again?, La Dama?, no, well, you know the one I mean, I threw up there more than anywhere else on the trip, I'm afraid I'm always going on about bodily functions, right?, hospital turns you into a body, the thing is we stopped too often that day, and it was so late there was no choice but to end up there, in Región, I was starting to see double, my legs felt shaky, I hated the idea of taking you to that dump, I was worried about you and I was worried about Pedro, to be on the safe side I tipped the security guard, a ridiculous amount, I gave him, enough for him to change the upholstery for us, and as we were going in I, ah, one other thing, the Internet at the motel did work, there was a gizmo behind reception, but, how can I put it, I was worried it would suddenly open up a load of porn pages, stupid, huh?, I sound like my mother, as if you weren't able to watch anything you like at home, do you watch porn already, son?, and will you like the same things as me?, the weird thing is that right there, in the bar in that dump, I know you and I had a memorable moment, it was, I was paying, right?, you still hadn't finished your dessert, and I could see, Lito, that you didn't want to, or to go to bed, or anything, and while I was waiting for the change I started looking round at the guys in the bar, some of them were really young, and suddenly it struck me I would never see you that way, at that age, leaning on a bar, and then I had, I don't know, a sort of attack from the future and I thought: Well, if I can't wait, then why not now, and I went over and asked if you wanted a drink, I swear I would have let you have anything, whisky, tequila, vodka, anything, and you ordered a Fanta, and it was fantastic, maybe this was why we made the trip, to have a Fanta in a motel with prostitutes, and then everything was worth it, until that disturbed man came over, that phony magician.

Look, I had to, I have to tell you what that man was after, I know it annoyed you us walking off like that, which is why I'm telling you this, even if it makes me want to throw up again, anyway, maybe you remember, who did he speak to first?, or rather, who did he touch first?, it was you, Lito, he fondled your arm, just a little, not much, and afterward he spoke to me, playing the joker, typical, I don't think he realized I was your father to start with, I dread to imagine what he thought then, that's why I said out loud: come along, *son*, but it was no good, the son of a bitch didn't stop, he went on talking to you, like he didn't believe me, or worse, like I, look, I swear, I was about to smash the guy's face in right there, to stamp on his ribs and crack his head open, I could see it, I tell you, I had it all worked out, exactly where I'd ram my fist, how to grab the chair and which part of his body I'd slam the chair legs into, everything, everything, I was a split second away, and then I realized I couldn't do that in front of you, I'm always telling you not to fight, poor kid, but to outsmart your schoolmates if one of them picks on you, so how the hell was I going to explain this?, well, there it is, now I've told you.

Ah, and another thing, next time someone picks on you at school, smash his face in for me, understood?, because on top of all that, the next morning the guy, it's unbelievable, I don't know if you noticed, when we went down to—.

They come in, they go out, they adjust this, they adjust that, I've no idea what they're giving me, I don't even ask anymore, it's humiliating, all that's left is for them to put me in nappies, I didn't want this, why doesn't your mum come and take me out of here?, why don't the visitors look me in the eye?, the worst of it is that I've learnt nothing from all this, what I feel is bitterness, before, how can I put it, I thought suffering was of some use, like a set of scales, if you follow me, a bit of suffering in exchange for a conclusion, weakness in exchange for some knowledge, crap, it's all crap, and besides, how vain can you be?, as if pain could be organized, no, pain is pure, it has no purpose, if there's one thing I can tell you for sure, son, it's this, don't teach yourself how to suffer, don't ever learn, look, from the moment they diagnose you, the world immediately splits into two, the camp of the living and the camp of those who are soon going to die, everyone starts treating you like you're no longer a member of their club, you belong to the other club now, as soon as I realized this I didn't want to say anything to anyone, I didn't want pity, I just wanted some time, at work, for example, if you talk about it at work, your colleagues stop telling you their problems, they stop asking you to do things even though you are still able to, they stop telling you about their plans for next year, in short, they erase you from the club's topics, it's not just the illness, the others take your future away from you, too, even your family, you know?, they don't consult you about anything, you're no longer a relative, you're just a shared problem, and in a hospital, well, what can I say?, it's even more obvious in here, the living watch the dying, son, that's basically what happens in this fucking place, I want to leave here, I want to piss myself in my own home, the living watch the dying, yes, or now that I think of it, there's a third club in here, a club whose members believe they can be saved, there's a narrow bridge between the other two, right?, and that bridge is filled with people in gowns, arms outstretched, arses bare.

When you're bedridden, you watch visitors come and go like in a play, a lousy play, right?, they all come over, act with you for a while, say goodbye, and then make their exits, and you, the supposed main character, are left wondering where they go to, what they do, what they talk about among themselves, and although you clearly remember that normal life isn't like this, you picture their days filled with fascinating activities, and so you envy them, loathe them, you want to see them in your shoes, to do them harm, infect them, until the door into the room opens again and you feel grateful, it's truly unbearable to feel thankful to people you know you will never be able to do any favours for, after chatting with your visitors, having a laugh with them, once they've all gone, you notice for a moment that you feel relieved, you were almost yearning for this, yearning to relax, to adopt your true face, right?, the face of a condemned man, but you don't want to be alone for too long either, and so after a while you start to miss the daily performance, and the light begins to fade, and the corridor grows still, and unless you're lucky and you sleep all right, you start counting how many hours it is until you hear the breakfast noises, understand?, at night I stare into space, and your mother watches me very intently, as if she were trying, I don't know, to guess what lofty thoughts I'm having, it isn't so easy to think in here, you don't always feel strong enough, so, for instance, I often reflect about taking a dump, but I don't tell your mum that, I don't say to her: I was reflecting about taking a little dump, I tell her I'm not reflecting about anything, it sounds better, although, to be honest, it shouldn't, because when you're in here, taking a dump is more important than almost anything else, and how itchy your back is, damn it, lying in these beds, you realize the depth of the body, the soul, or whatever, is completely secondary, you put it on hold straight away, your physical reality is the most pressing, complex thing, full of mysteries even for the doctors, I understand less and less about what's down there, below the sheets, I look at it as if it were someone else's, and that other thing, I mean, that, it doesn't seem like it's mine either, or maybe it does, I still notice it occasionally, but I can't even bring myself to touch it, I don't want to touch anything that's part of my body, everything in my body is my enemy now, this is what it is to be dead.

I think I'm about to contradict myself, let's see, no, because you can't imagine how much time I have to reflect now that my time is running out, somehow I never stop reflecting even when I'm asleep, yes, I'm contradicting myself, there, in my head, everything goes very fast, one minute is a luxury for the mind, at least when your back isn't itching, your mum just called, she's on her way, she's a bit late, our marriage hasn't been perfect, I expect you're already aware of that, knowing I'm going to die makes me love her more, I discovered love when I got sick, it's like I'm a hundred and twenty, I'm still young, a youth of a hundred and twenty, and shall I tell you something?, I don't deserve this love, because before I knew I was going to die, I didn't appreciate how to feel it, sometimes I think illness is a punishment, and the more your mother looks after me the more indebted to her I feel, and I'm not going to be able to repay that debt, she keeps telling me no, what nonsense, we do these things out of love, but debts of love also exist, anyone who denies that is fooling themselves, and such debts never go away, at most we conceal them, like I am now.

Electronic kangaroo, on the phone today you told me about your football match with the neighbours, about the cool trainers your granddad bought you, the concert you went to with grandma, how you beat the record in I don't know what, do you know what your granddad did when I started dating his little girl?, he bought me a pair of slippers, silk slippers, he explained very courteously, for when I wanted to sleep at his house, great, hurrah, the problem is that the damn slippers were his size, not mine, they were tiny on me, it was impossible for me to wear them, there's liberals for you, I'm so glad you're having fun, I've told you how busy I am, how great I feel now I'm over the flu, about all the deliveries I'm making for Uncle Juanjo while he's on holiday, I tell you about trips I'm not taking, places I'm not seeing, roads I'm not driving on, one of these days I'm going to have an accident, and that accident is going to separate us cleanly, Lito, I want you to remember us like this, travelling together, now all the memories, even the silliest ones, give off a light, like those little screens you're so . . .

Lito

Mum calls again. I guess she's missing us a lot. We've spoken three times today already. When we got up. When we stopped for lunch at Santa María de la Reina. And now we're arriving at Salto Grande with the delivery. I miss her as well. But not when she asks me. Funny, that.

Oh my angel, Mum says, no, nothing, are you all right?, are you having a good time?, are you eating some fruit?, what about dad?, hasn't he driven enough for today?, why doesn't he take a nap?, how much further is it?, is the weather still nice?, do you know how much I love you, honey?, do you?

Mum makes noises like she's blowing her nose. Ma, I say, are you crying?

Me? she answers laughing, no, son, what makes you think that!, it's just a silly cold, all this air-conditioning!, well, no, nothing, I was just calling to, I saw the time and thought, bah, you'd be there already, where's the delivery again?, in Santa María de la?, wait, no, that was at noon, well, I just wanted, how about salads? (yes, almost every day, I lie), well, all right, but it should be every day, okay? (of course, Mum, I answer), anyway, when you eat hamburgers and things like that at night you don't sleep so well, they're very hard to digest, do you understand, my love?, that's why, do you know what the best thing would be?, if you ordered at most (we overtake a black VW and return to our lane, the VW accelerates, overtakes us, and pulls back in front of Pedro, Dad swears under his breath, brakes and puts the indicator on again to overtake), is something wrong, angel?, what's wrong? (nothing, Mum, nothing, I say), are you sure, honey? (I swear, I answer), well, as I was saying, I don't want to be a pain, really I don't, but I'd prefer it if for dessert you (we overtake the black Volkswagen again, and this time Dad stays in the other lane and accelerates, he accelerates a lot, until the Volkswagen grows small in the mirror and disappears, wow!, awesome!, Pedro's super fast even though he's big!, and suddenly the clouds start moving, they're going away, it must be because we're driving much faster now), sounds good, my love?, do you promise? (I promise, Mum, I say, I love you tons).

Mum asks me to pass her over to Dad. He slows down and takes the phone. He's holding the wheel with one hand. I don't understand why he never plugs the phone into Pedro's speaker. That's what Uncle Juanjo does. Why do Mum and Dad really like doing the things they tell me people shouldn't do? Dad only says, yes, no, well, aha, I see, later. It's hard to tell what they're talking about. I hope they're not fighting.

I straighten my cap in the mirror. It's a bit big for my head. But it looks awesome. The magician said I'd changed. And it's true with the cap on I look different. More like I'm ten or more. Maybe that was the trick. One thing's for sure. This cap is special. I wish I could've asked the magician where he got it. It's a lot like the one Stallone wears in, what's that movie called? The one on TV at the motel the other day? In that movie Stallone is a trucker like Uncle Juanjo. Well, not like Uncle Juanjo. Driving a truck is much more exciting in the movie. In real life it's okay. But sometimes you get bored. Or your back hurts. Stallone's back never hurt. Of course he trains all the time. And his back muscles are super strong. In the movie he stops to arm wrestle fat guys with moustaches. And he beats all of them. That's what I like about Stallone. He always beats bigger and taller guys. And he teaches his son. At first you think he's a sissy. But in the end he learns. I wish I had a Dad like that. I mean, my Dad's awesome. But I wish he'd teach me how to arm wrestle the jerks at school. I don't think he can now. He gets more tired because of the virus. Stallone doesn't get ill. But Dad still has loads of strength. Totally. I tried to lift his backpack yesterday. Oof. No way.

I imagine we're in the school gym. I'm arm wrestling the jerks and I'm wearing my cap. I twist their arms. Lift them up in the air. I make them look ridiculous. Lying on the floor. Crying like wimps. And my friends all clap like crazy. I try to imagine it and I can't. The images go all fuzzy. My mind goes blank in the middle of the arm wrestle. Or else suddenly I see they're winning and they're bending my arm back and making fun of me. This image is really clear. Them making fun of me. Kicking me. Spitting at me. Then I imagine something else. I imagine a huge truck honking its horn loud. It smashes through the school fence. Destroys the gym. Drives over everybody. Squashing their heads. One by one. Crack. Crack. Crack. And I feel better. And I look in the mirror. Hey, says Dad, aren't you going to take off that horrible cap?

The delivery takes forever. I thought when we got there, we unloaded and that was it. The guy Dad knows isn't at the warehouse. It's a different guy. And he complains about how late we are. Dad raises his voice. The other guy threatens to make him come back tomorrow. And to send a complaint or something. Dad gets furious. He looks like he might hit the guy even. I'd love that. Then he calms down. He tells me to wait in the truck. And he gets out. I wait for a bit. Dad takes ages. This bit of the warehouse is dark. I can hardly see anything from up here. Just piles and piles of crates wrapped in plastic. I look for the phone to play mini-golf. Too bad. I think Dad's taken it. Oof. I'm bored. I press the horn. Two workmen look at me from a freight lift. They keep going up. And they disappear. The freight lift sounds like a normal lift. It makes more noise when it goes up than when it comes down. The workmen go down again. After that, I don't know. Suddenly I hear the truck door. I open my eyes. I see Dad arranging some papers. I stretch my arms. Everything okay? I ask. Bah, he sighs, money talks.

It's getting late. We drive past industrial units. We can see Salto Grande in the distance. Sometimes we pass other trucks. We say hello turning Pedro's headlights on and off. There's a ton of machinery. Cranes. Bulldozers. Diggers. Just like the ones on TV only dirtier. We stop at a traffic light. I can see a crane hook inside the sun. It's like a claw on a sticker. If they lower the crane it'll get dark all of a sudden. Dad's phone rings. He doesn't answer. We speed up.

We circle the outskirts of the town. Dad asks me if we should look for a motel or start driving home. What if we go in for a bit? I say. In where? he asks, the town? Best not, son, there are too many hills. So what? I say. So nothing, he answers, I'm a bit tired that's all. But it's right in front of us! I complain, what if I never come back? Dad stays silent. He stares at the road. He blows air through his nose. He crinkles his face. I think he's going to say yes.

It was time we got out of that cab! The town is awesome. White. Totally white. With tons of shadows. Full of tiny streets and steps. It's like a maze in 3-D. Sometimes you don't know if you're going up or down. Dad's lazy today. He doesn't want to lose another race so he suggests we play the step game. These are the rules. When we pass some steps I have to guess how many there are. Run and count them as quickly as I can. And come back and tell Dad exactly how many. If I'm right to within ten steps I get a point. If not, he gets a point. The first to get ten points wins. It must be really cool living here. I run. Count steps. Go up. Come down. I've already got seven points. It's not so easy. Sometimes I cheat. Not much. Just a bit. I leave out two or three steps. Never more. The walls are very pretty, they turn red. Orange. Pink. It's quite windy now. Dad calls me from the bottom of the steps. I can't hear him properly. I go up, and down. I run, I count. I try not to trip over. I've got nine points so far.

We sit down at some plastic tables. There are old people and kids with dogs in the square. I'm pouring with sweat but super happy. Dad coughs. I order a Coke with a slice of lemon. He asks for a bottle of mineral water. And he takes an allergy pill. I drink my Coke in one go. I ask Dad if I can order another. I'm sure he'll say no. He doesn't like me having too many fizzy drinks. But this time he says yes. Mum would be angry. Dad keeps coughing. He tells me the air in Salto Grande is full of pollen. I tip my glass. The ice cubes bounce off my nose. I imagine I'm a spaceship and they're meteorites crashing into me. Is there ice in space? Or is space made of ice? I saw a documentary about glaciers the other day. But if so, then how do spaceships fly? Or maybe they drill through space as they fly? My tummy is full of bubbles. My tummy could do with a drill. I burp and laugh. I ask if we're leaving yet. Dad says he prefers to stay here a bit longer. I fold my arms. I'm starting to feel bored. I look around. I see a poster with the Internet sign. I ask if I can go. Dad can't see the poster I'm pointing to very well. He looks at all the people around us. He hesitates. He tells me on no account to go off any-where else. He'll be watching the door. And he gives me a few coins. Cool! He's soft today.

I go into my e-mail. There's a message from Mum in the in-box. Another from Edu with photos. And a ton of spam. I delete the spam and read the messages. I reply to Mum. I look for Edu in chat. He's not there. I look for Pablo. For Rafa and Josema. They're not there either. I guess they're all on holiday. I think of trying to find Marina. I like Marina. And she's almost got tits. She loves writing in chat. She says our classmates are all stupid and don't even know how to say hello properly. I should practise first. I'll try another day. I sign out of e-mail. I start listening to stuff on YouTube. The sound sucks. I get up and ask for some headphones. They tell me they're all in use. I sit down again. What do I do now? Suddenly I remember the movie. What was it called? I type: stallone + truck. It comes up almost straight away. I find out something totally weird. In some countries it's called *Falcon*. In others *I am the Falcon*. And in English it's called *Over the Top*. Not that I know much English. But *top* definitely isn't falcon. And *over* isn't either. What have falcons to do with trucks? Maybe Stallone transported birds in his truck. I don't think so. Actually you never know what he transports. The only thing he takes with him is his cap. And his sissy of a son. I go into Google Translate. I type: ober the, no, over the top. Two results. *Sobre la tapa* and *por encima*. The truth is the English title doesn't make much sense either. Even though I've seen it several times. Who decides what movies are called?

Polyglot lizard, I hear as someone pulls my cap over my eyes, time to go? I push my cap up. I turn round. I ask Dad: What's a polyglot? He gives me a kiss and says: Search.

Elena

The 15th at 19.50h.

The 15th, 7:50 p.m.

The fifteenth at ten to eight.

Do these numbers mean anything?

Do I understand what has happened if I say "the 15th" or "19.50h"? Was reality different at 19.49h? Did the world change during that minute? Why do I reread these figures over and over, I read "the 15th", I read "19.50h" and I still don't understand what they mean?

I was going to write, but didn't.

No desire to read.

Not today either.

✧ ✧ ✧

It happened like this.

I had just had a shower. I was dressing to go to spend the night at the hospital, when the phone rang. It was Juanjo. He spoke quickly or I understood slowly. The monitor. The serum. The oxygen. The two nurses who had just come in. He couldn't get his words out. He was having great difficulty breathing.

I hung up. I'll never be able to forgive myself for the first thing that entered my head.

I thought about finishing drying my hair.

My hair. My head.

I ordered a cab. It didn't come. I didn't wait. I walked out of the house. I crossed in the wrong place. I thrust myself between a lady and a cab for hire. The lady ticked me off. I took umbrage. I muttered something about artificial respiration. I climbed into the car. It drove off. There was traffic everywhere. We were going slowly. Sometimes no faster than the pedestrians. I saw the numbers changing on the taximeter. Suddenly I got out. I got out of the car and I ran. My phone rang. I nearly passed out. I answered terrified. It wasn't Juanjo. It was the cab company. They wanted to know where I was. The driver had been waiting for me for some time outside my house. I yelled at the woman from the cab company. I kept yelling at her as I ran. I poured abuse on her. People stared at me. The woman hung up. I kept running. I was dripping with sweat. My legs were stinging. My entire body was throbbing. A mix of burning and cold rose up my throat. I thought I was about to spit out a lump of something. Something that rattled. As I ran I thought about Mario. At last. Completely. Only about him. His mouth. His nose. His breath. His breathing. I tried to help him. I tried to breathe with him. I choked. We choked. I imagined my mouth on his mouth. My lungs and his. I imagined I was blowing. Blowing hard enough to raise him off the bed, to propel me to the hospital.

In the end I arrived in time.

We never arrive in time.

That is what happened on the day of the fifteenth before ten to eight. The night was worse.

Someone had to call the funeral home to buy the coffin. And the newspapers to dictate the death notice. Two simple, inconceivable tasks. So intimate, so remote. Buying the coffin and dictating the death notice. No one teaches you these things. How to get sick, care for, declare terminally ill, say goodbye, hold a wake, bury, cremate. I wonder what the hell they do teach us.

First it was the funeral parlour. Or, to be precise, the funeral parlours. Because there are many. A great many. All offering different deals. The hospital itself furnishes you with the contact numbers. As if this were part of the treatment. With the same efficiency with which they give enemas.

One parlour charges less for the coffin, but extra for the transport to the cemetery. Another gives you free transport to the cemetery, but charges more to hire the venue for the wake. Another gives you a discount on the venue, but doesn't carry a cheaper range of coffins. Yet another seems more costly, but their price includes taxes. Then you realize the other prices that seemed more reasonable didn't include tax. And you are back at square one. And the queues of widows and orphans come and go. If dying is just another procedure, I prefer the rituals of any exotic tribe.

As you dial number after number, enquire, write down, have misgivings, and hang up, you never cease to feel, not even for a second, like the stingiest creature on earth. Incapable of offering the person you love, the person you didn't save, a decent repose. You suspect you are committing an atrocity, bargaining at a moment like this. That it would be nobler to bow to this extortion in silence and allow yourself to grieve. But, at the same time, as though you were being stabbed in the back, you resent the crass opportunism of this business, the bloodthirsty profiting from your loss. So you try again to find a figure that seems reasonable (how much is a reasonable death? what is a costly corpse?), a price, let's say, that doesn't oblige your corpse to claim riches he didn't have. And you are back to square one with the phone calls, while the lines of widows and orphans keep coming and going.

In the end, in the middle of a call to one of the parlours, I felt bad about all my bartering, and signed up to the first deal they offered, I gave them my personal details, my credit card number, thanked them, hung up, and instantly regretted having accepted a price Mario never would have accepted.

Dictating the death notice was no easier. Dictating it: announcing the death of a loved one in the third person. Imagining someone is reading it as you are drafting it. Pretending you don't know your husband has died, and that you are finding out from this announcement. He, in the third person, your beloved, in the second person, who will never exist in the first person again. Grammar doesn't believe in reincarnation. Literature does.

I must dictate the death notice straight away, they told me, or I'd have to wait another day, they explained. If I didn't have the text prepared, they lamented, there was no choice but to do it on the spot. The newspaper was closing, they informed me. There was enough time to insert a normal death notice, a religious one, they corrected themselves, one that prays for the soul of the, and so on, they recited. But there isn't time, madam, they said hurriedly, to start reinventing the format.

As I improvised the text of the first death notice, I was tempted to give my name in place of Mario's.

I had to dictate the final death notice to a trainee with a twang, because everyone in the office had gone home. And it was a question, he said, of *middits*. If we didn't send it off straight away, the notice wouldn't *get enderred*. When the trainee said *get enderred*, I heard *interred*. The notice wouldn't get interred. Afterward, he offered to read it back to me, to *bake* sure the text was *coddect*. I listened to it delivered in his voice, in the twangy voice of someone who was probably the nicest of all those who had answered me that night, I listened to my death notice full of apparent misspellings and impossible blunders. Then I went into paroxysms of laughter, a succession of muscular contractions over which I had no control, as though I had become tangled up in an electric cable, and the trainee with the twang asked me if I was all right, and I said yes and became electrocuted with laughter, and one of my brothers-in-law handed me a glass of water and a sedative.

I went outside to get some fresh air. I noticed no difference between outside and inside. I called my parents' house. First I spoke to Lito. I told him we would see each other very soon. That in a few days' time, Mum was going to drive over and pick him up, and that on the way home we were going to stop and eat a double hamburger. I didn't do a very good job of pretending. Then I asked him to let me speak to his grandma. When my mum took the receiver, I cried for a while. We didn't speak. Even when she is silent, my mum knows what to say. I won't make old bones knowing as much as she. Or I won't make old bones. Afterward, I called my sister. Because of the time difference, I woke her up. She gave me her condolences in a voice thick with sleep, and talked to me about flights, stopovers, dates. Then I called a few women friends. They found the right words to comfort me. Two of them took taxis over. Suddenly it occurred to me that they were able to comfort me so effectively because they'd been practising what they would say to me for months. That made me feel worse. Then I thought about Ezequiel. I sent him a text message and turned off my phone.

My brothers-in-law were waiting for me at the entrance to the crematorium. They were arguing when I got there. The undertakers had just arrived, but there was a problem: they had brought us a casket with a Catholic cross. An enormous crucifix stretching the whole length of the lid. I assured them I had ordered a plain one. In fact I wasn't so sure. I had the feeling I was dreaming every conversation. Juanjo thought the casket with the crucifix was perfect, just what their parents would have wanted. His younger brother disagreed. The middle brother thought I should be the one to decide. What should we do, then, Madam? the employee from the funeral parlour asked. I replied without thinking, as though someone were dictating to me: Let God's will be done. Juanjo took it as sarcasm and walked off. I heard him murmur: And on top of everything else, she blasphemes.

I prefer not to think about the wake. Silence. Family. Crematorium.

I look up *wake* in the dictionary. The third entry is absurd: "Spend the night watching over the deceased." As if, instead of watching over our guests, we were attending to the dead.

Absurd and precise.

I hadn't read a single line since that day. What for. I always thought books, all books, spoke of my life. What would be the point of reading about something I no longer care about.

But yesterday, in a drawer in his bedside table, I found a novel Mario had left half-finished. And I felt duty bound to read it from there to the end. It was a novel by Hemingway, an author I loathe. I started exactly where he had left off. It was strange working out the other half.

Today I went back on the pills.

I cried stones.

Since Lito is back, it may seem like a contradiction, but Mario's absence is more noticeable. The time I spent here alone was a kind of simulation. Its unusualness postponed the return to routine. What pains me most are my conversations with my son, when we talk about death in the kitchen.

He asks me how such a big truck could get crushed. I tell him sometimes big things break more.

He asks me why Pedro looks the same as before, if he had such a big accident. I tell him his uncle did a really good job fixing him up in the workshop.

He asks me if he can go on another trip in Pedro. I tell him maybe when he is older.

He asks if he can go and play ball in the park. I tell him he can. But my son doesn't leave the kitchen. He remains there, seated, staring at me.

I have thrown away his clothes. Except for his shirts, I'm not sure why. I stuffed all his belongings in bin bags, almost without looking at them, and I put them out with the rubbish. I went upstairs. I made dinner. After putting Lito to bed, I ran down into the street. The rubbish bins were already empty.

A colleague had recommended *The Foolish Children* by Ana María Matute. I was slightly put off by the title. Now I understand why she kept insisting I read it. Death and childhood are rarely dealt with at the same time. We adults, not to mention mothers, prefer childhood to be innocent, pleasant, tender. In brief, the opposite of real life. I wonder whether, by shielding them from pain, we aren't compounding their future suffering.

"He was a peculiar child," I underline as I reflect on what Lito's teachers tell me, "who never lost his belt, or ruined his shoes, or had scabs on his knees, or got his fingers dirty," they tell me he doesn't go to the playground during break time, he doesn't seem interested in playing with the others, and is always drawing in a notebook or staring out of the window, "he was another child, with no dreams of horses and no fear of the dark," and that sometimes he goes quiet, sits very still, and frowns, as though he were about to come to some conclusion he never reaches.

But I don't care about my qualms, I want to look after him anyway, protect him from everything, embrace him in the playground, talk to him as if he were a baby, lie to him, spoil him, erase for him every trace of death, tell him: Not you, son, never.

Last night I dreamt I came home (except the house was bigger and it had a garden with orange trees), I opened the door and Mario greeted me wearing a costume. There was a party, and all the guests were dressed as skeletons. Someone handed me a costume. I put it on. Then Mario told me his death had been a joke, and the two of us burst into fits of laughter, violent, convulsive laughter, and with our guffaws the skeletons slowly began to fall apart.

Each morning, when I open my eyes, I see the hospital. Everything is there, like a sticky sheet. The monitor. The drips. The oxygen mask. The shadows under Mario's eyes. His defeated smile. Good morning, sentinel, he would say to me.

Who was in greater need of that treatment: him or me? Was I experimenting with my hope through another person's body? How could I have let them take him? What were we doing in the hospital: attending to him or detaining him? Were the doctors taking care of him or their procedures, their conscience? Did I keep him there in order to put off my loneliness?

Again and again I go back to the image of his diminished body, his sagging muscles, his half-open mouth. I reproach myself for not remembering him at his best. I keep telling myself it is unfair to insist on this final portrait of him. But the wonderful, strong Mario doesn't need my help. And it is as though the other, weak Mario were still asking me to care for him in retrospect. Sometimes I think that, by continually going back to him, this suffering Mario will finally be able to rest, will feel accepted.

When a book tells me something I was trying to say, I feel the right to appropriate its words, as if they had once belonged to me and I were taking them back.

"She has already started to wear sunglasses indoors, like a celebrity widow," I was startled to read in a short story by Lorrie Moore, sometimes I do the same, using my photophobia as an excuse, so that Lito won't see my eyes. "From where will her own strength come? From some philosophy? From some frigid little philosophy?" Actually, I don't get my strength from reading, but I do understand my weakness.

"She is neither stalwart nor realistic," if I were stalwart I would surrender to loss forever, that would serve me right; as for realism, illness ends up turning it into daily ravings, so lucidity and hallucination become all mixed up, "and has trouble with basic concepts, such as the one that says events move in one direction only and do not jump up, turn around, and take themselves back," events in life never move forward, they rewind ceaselessly, they repeat themselves, wiping out previous versions, the way we used to do with cassette tapes, the way Mario did with these recordings I am incapable of listening to without self-medicating, and which I have no idea when I should give to Lito.

"The Husband begins too many of his sentences with 'What if,'" I begin each day rewinding my actions, wondering what would have happened if I had taken better care of him, what if I had realized sooner that he wasn't well, what if I had convinced him to see the doctor sooner, what if I had accepted his initial reaction, what if I had agreed to his idea of rejecting treatment from the start, what if I had acknowledged that it wasn't working, what if I had allowed him to say goodbye to us at home, what if we had told our son the truth, what if, what if. No one is saved from the "What if." No "What if" saves anyone.

❖ ❖ ❖

He called.

Today. He called.

Him.

He said (yesterday, Ezequiel) he hadn't wanted to disturb me before. (Disturb me.) That, out of respect, he had chosen to keep silent. (Respect. His for me.) Are we going to see each other? he asked. (See each other. Him and me.) I don't know, I replied. You don't know or you don't want to? he asked. I don't know if I want to, I replied. And I hung up.

What offended me exactly? His untimely reappearance? But everything about Ezequiel is untimely. This was precisely what excited me about him.

Or did it offend me that he took so long? That he didn't insist from day one? Did his respect bother me? Or his discretion? Or the possibility that he had forgotten me? That he was capable of repressing the urge to call me, to see me, to defile me?

Yet if he had begun calling me on day one, what would I have done? I would have hung up on him. And so?

And so, here I am. This is me.

What are you writing, darling? asks my mother, who is staying with us for a few days. Nothing, I reply, nothing. It's good for you to express yourself, she says smiling. And she goes out, leaving me a cup of tea. I wonder whether my mother expresses herself.

Did I reach a point where I wanted Mario to die? I woke up with this question. I woke Lito up with this question in mind. My son opened his eyes and I had the feeling he could read it. I hugged him, kissed him, buried myself in him, swallowed my tears, I told him I had a cold.

As Lito walked in to school, I watched him turn his head toward the car.

What is the difference between taking pity on a sick man and deserting him?

I threw up between classes.

Ezequiel has not called.

"It is a commonly held idea," I protest through a novel by Javier Marías, "that what has happened should be less painful to us than what is happening, or that things are easier to bear when they are over with," and it is the opposite: while things are happening we have to deal with them, and the anaesthetic comes precisely from dealing with them. "This is equivalent to thinking that someone dead is less serious than someone dying," someone dying at least asks you for help, justifies your pain. "There are those who say to me: *keep the good memories and forget the end*," what sort of advice is that?, don't we remember books, movies, love affairs partly because of their endings, largely because of their endings?, what degree of forgetfulness does it require to remember a beginning without its end? "They are well-meaning people," they are idiots, "who don't realize that every memory has been tainted," grief spreads through memory like an environmental disaster.

"The effects far outlast the patience of those who appear willing to listen," they call me, ask how I am, and, when I tell them the truth, they are disappointed or try to contradict me, as though it were wrong of me to go on being upset when I have such loyal friends, such steadfast relatives. "Every misfortune has a social sell-by date, nobody is made for contemplating suffering," or happiness for that matter: the only thing we tolerate in others is monotony, the tendency not to exist, "this spectacle is bearable for a time, while there is still some turmoil, and a certain possibility of prominence for those watching who feel indispensable, playing the role of saviour," but why don't you call us when you need help? they complain, what are friends for? what is family for? They are confusing SOS with OSS, what I call Obligatory Sentimental Service.

When someone you slept with dies, you begin to doubt their body and yours. The once touched body withdraws from the hypothesis of a re-encounter, it becomes unverifiable, may not have existed. Your own body loses substance. Your muscles fill with vapour, they don't know what it was they were clutching. When someone with whom you have slept dies, you never sleep in the same way again. Your body doesn't let itself go when it is in bed, your arms and legs open as though clinging to the rim of a well, trying not to fall in. It insists on waking up earlier, on making sure at least it possesses itself. When someone with whom you have slept dies, the caresses you gave their skin change direction, they go from relived presence to posthumous experience. There is a hint of salvation and a hint of violation about imagining that skin now. A posteriori necrophilia. The beauty that was once with us remains stuck to us. As does its fear. Its hurt.

I promise not to write until he calls.

This is what you get for being proud.

For being proud and a whore.

But, but.

He called. Again.

And not only that. He also begged me.

He told me he dreamt of seeing me again. Incessantly, he said. In a serene voice. I didn't think this was enough. I refused. He asked what he had done wrong. I laughed. I asked him if his question was serious. He kept saying yes, in an increasingly anxious voice. I told him not to worry so much, because he had a legion of widows to console. He asked me if I was trying to humiliate him. I asked him if he was trying to humiliate himself.

Then he wept. Ezequiel wept.

I hadn't felt such distinct pleasure for a long time.

Confronted with death, our emotions tense up, stretch, almost snap. They veer from paralysing pain to hyperactive euphoria.

The other's death throes are more or less fleeting. Not these conflicting emotions. As though the survivors' inner arc had collapsed, leaving them capable of either extreme. Of the greatest empathy and the greatest cruelty. Animal loyalties and wartime treason.

In his recording, I can't stop thinking about this, Mario said that debts of love also exist, and that we are fooling ourselves if we deny it. He said these debts can't be repaid, but they can be silenced. And that I, if I understood correctly, did I? had hushed up his debts, so he was going to hush up mine.

I lock myself in the bathroom to listen to this passage, I hear his voice again, his voice talking to himself, and I can't believe this voice has no person, a first person without anybody there, that my son is being spoken to by his father and yet Lito doesn't have a father, that my husband talks about me and yet in the bathroom there is no one but me.

What did Mario know? This doubt weighs on me.

Doubt, debt.

He continued calling, and I picking up. I told him: No. And I hung up. He called again. I picked up again and I said: No. And I hung up again.

The only good thing about this unhealthy pursuit was that all of a sudden, after several months, I noticed I was getting moist. For the first time since I have been alone. And I was able to touch myself again. And while I was feeling, to cry. Orgasms, none.

The next time he called I told him to go down on his knees and beg if he really wanted to talk to me. Because I needed to know whether my shame and his were comparable. He said he understood me. I said I doubted that very much. He asked if Lito was at home. I told him it was none of his business. He implored me, in a very gentle voice, just to answer yes or no. I hesitated. I began to murmur: No, but. The conversation ended.

A few minutes later the doorbell rang.

I was pleased to see Ezequiel there, kneeling in the doorway. He looked like a religious portrait. I guessed he was sincere, because he didn't even attempt to come in. He remained still. Silent. Gazing up at me. Like a tame animal. He looked off-colour. He had thinner shoulders and more pronounced cheekbones. I said to him: You've lost weight. He took this as a compliment and his face lit up. He made as if to get up. I immediately added: I don't like it. He shrank back. It is the only time I have ever seen a man who is kneeling fall to his knees.

Realizing he couldn't convince me, Ezequiel started to put on his Dr. Escalante face. As though I had a problem and he could diagnose it. I stood firm. When he realized I was serious, that I had no intention this time of letting him inside my house, Ezequiel clutched one of my legs. Only one. I didn't move a muscle.

Ezequiel let go. He placed his hands on the floor and stood up. It took him some effort. He stared straight at me. At that moment, I expected him to suffer an attack of wounded pride. To raise his voice to me, to insult me, or something. But no: he began to snivel. And I knew that if he was capable of doing this to himself, then he was capable of doing anything to me.

I started closing the door. On the other side, Ezequiel began to stammer that he needed me.

I held the door.

Without looking out I replied: That's exactly what I wanted to hear. Now leave my house. And never call again.

I continued closing the door. The mat in the entrance made

a noise as it dragged along the floor. I had the impression of
sweeping something.

Strange to be writing again. The last time was quite a while ago.
In the meantime, I have had to reconcile myself to a few things.
The first of these being the fact that the world kept going round
as though nothing had happened.

Best not to elaborate too much on my classroom routine (when
I don't teach I get bored, when I teach I get frustrated), the val-
ues of my colleagues (how is it possible to teach literature and
only read sports magazines?), the hysteria of my female students
(will they never stop falling for the boys who treat them the worst?),
the hormonal frenzy of my male students (some of them still look
at my legs, and at this stage I must confess it is almost a relief),
the dilemma of exams (if I give them good grades I feel irresponsible, if I give them bad grades I feel guilty), the equations at the
end of the month (I increasingly check the price of things in the
supermarket), my quandary about Mario's pension (using that
money depresses me), the emptiness, the emptiness.

Or taking charge of Mario's ashes, for example. This is what
the people at the cemetery said to me. They said once the storage
period had expired, I must *take charge of* them. This was the language they used. *Store them*, they said. Can ashes belong to someone? And, more importantly, are ashes someone?

His half ashes, to be precise: half for me, the other half for
his brothers. They wanted to plant a tree, I wanted to scatter
them in the sea. In the end we decided to share them out. *In two
equal parts*, we said. The family is a scavenging animal.

I have always found going to cemeteries difficult. We grow
up believing there are only one mother and father, until we

discover millions more there, all of them dead. I wonder where my parents want to be buried. Why do I never talk to them about this, to my sister? We all live in an ellipsis.

Mario and I once discussed our funerals. We spoke of such things when they had no meaning. As soon as they grew in importance, I was incapable of talking about them. Oddly enough so was he. I don't know whether this was an omission or a decision. Perhaps he wanted to let me choose. But this choice weighs too heavily on me: I would have preferred to do his will. It would have been more generous to allow me to carry out his wishes than to bequeath me all this uncertainty.

I tried to broach it with Lito in the gentlest way possible (*gentle?*) in order to have his opinion. His reply touched me and left me confused, because he ultimately agreed with his uncles. He said he preferred a tree, because the roots could grow and grow under the soil and maybe one day, after many years, he would trip over them. I promised him we would go to plant it with Uncle Juanjo.

I wonder whether a dead person can have a *place*. Whether marking it preserves their memory or, in some way, curtails it. Who do these places really belong to? To the ones who remember. A place for the dead is a refuge for the living. Yet death, for me, must be more like the elements. In constant motion. A return to every place the departed went to or might have gone. I feel unable to *go* to Mario's death, because I live settled in it. Because it is diffused everywhere and nowhere. We will never know the whereabouts of our deceased.

A tree is motionless. The sea comes back. I was right.

But a tree grows. The sea doesn't. They were right.

But a tree grows old. The sea renews itself. I was right.

But you can embrace a tree. The sea is elusive. They were right.

But?

Yesterday I drove around all day with my half of the ashes, with Mario's dust on the seat beside me. I headed for the coast in a sort of receptive silence. As though I were listening to the passenger.

I wanted to remember the sea when I thought of him. To rinse away those final memories, wash his ailing body, flood that shitty hospital with salt.

I didn't know exactly where I was heading. I drove along the coast and waited for some sort of sign. No place spoke to me, or they all said the same. It would soon be getting dark. I started to panic. I had the impression the whole coast was turning its back on me.

As I kept driving, I realized that deep down I was trying to delegate the choice. To delegate it to anything that was beyond my will: chance, magic, the road, the urn. So I stopped the car.

I looked at the sea, including myself in it. And I thought of Mario. Not in sickness, not as the father of my son, not even as the youth I fell in love with at university. Not in the random coming together of a name, a body, a memory. I thought of him, or rethought him without me. As someone who might not have met me. Who might have lived a parallel life, and, although it sounds naïve, who might be born in a different place. At that moment I looked at the time and thought: Now. It didn't matter where. This was it, it was now. The ritual wasn't in a place, it was in the time spent searching for the ritual.

I took the first turning I came to. It was an ordinary beach, neither pretty nor ugly. It evoked no particular memories. I understood, I thought I understood, that places invaded by the past don't let anything else in. I stopped the car. I got out with the urn. I walked toward the seashore. I took off my shoes. I looked around. I saw a few joggers in the distance. I wasn't sure (this seems frivolous to me now, it seemed logical then) whether to keep undressing. One of the joggers started getting bigger. I preferred to wait until he had gone by. And in the meantime I, I did what? Tried to look natural? Gazing at the view with an urn in my arms? I guess this looked more conspicuous than getting naked. The jogger went by. I took off my skirt. I realized I hadn't waxed my legs. I stepped forward, I wet my feet. The sea was cold. The sky was burning hot. I glanced around me. On one side of the beach another jogger was approaching. I stepped back quickly, I walked away from the water, sat on the sand, and hid the urn between my legs. The jogger ran behind me. I turned to look at him, he looked at me, and disappeared into the distance. I stood up. I ran into the sea. This time I went in up to my waist, raising the urn above my head. I couldn't see the horizon very clearly, the sun was setting level with my eyes. I waded in further. The waves lapped at my breasts. The light was floating. Everything was haloed. I opened the urn. Only then did I notice the wind, plastering my hair to my face. How was I going to scatter the ashes? But it was too late for misgivings. I was where I should be: in a random place, at the precise moment. I dug my hand into the ashes. I touched them for the first time. They felt rougher and denser than I had expected. In short, they didn't look like ashes. Although I did feel they could contain Mario, or that Mario could fly away with them. I grasped a handful. I raised my arm. And I started.

I threw them into the air, they came back.

As they flew into my face, there was some kind of fulfilment. A, does this make sense?, funereal joy. I felt the current encircling me, and at the same time warning me of a boundary. The sun dipped to the edge. The light fell like a towel. Like the sky was sliding: that was the impression I had. I carried on emptying the urn. I imagined I was sowing the sea.

It wasn't sad. I scattered his ashes and pieced myself together. Now he can swim, I thought as I left the water.

Mario

. . . in Puerto del Este, I remember the esplanade, I remember the yachts, how they caught your attention, rich people always catch the attention, right?, whenever I see a yacht I think about who cleans the bathroom, and I remember the sun, the bicycles, I remember the people strolling in their swimming costumes, surrounded by light, happy, happy, like they weren't going to die, you ran through them, I remember.

For me the last day of our trip was, how can I explain, sad and at the same time a relief, do you understand?, we'd done it, no one could take that away from us, or could they, you'll think I'm crazy, but I got so nervous while you were swimming, I was watching you from the beach and thinking: what if he gets a cramp?, what if suddenly we lose this memory?, I swear, each time you put your head under the water, I swear, I stopped breathing, I looked at the men closest to me, I saw which ones were strongest, the ones I'd ask for help, because, you see, son, I can't swim, I was always too ashamed to tell you, and then your head bobbed up once more and I could breathe again, of course nothing happened to you, nothing could've happened, you were fearless.

The rest of the journey was more or less okay, we were late, your mother started calling and then there was that storm, what a downpour, right?, I was worried we'd miss dinner, and that dinner was important, in the end, I admit, I drove too fast, and, to make matters worse, on a wet road, risk is a strange thing, you think you're being careful, that you're protecting the things you most care about, and then you accelerate knowing you shouldn't, and then you regret it, and the next time you accelerate again, I was soaked when we arrived, out of breath, my head was pounding, but I made it, we made it, I think your Mum had had her doubts, she almost looked surprised, her face as she greeted us, she was crying, laughing, she kept hugging us, and yes, she had to heat up the joint, and the three of us made a toast, do you remember?, you even had some wine, and we told your Mum lots of stories, you elaborated everything, it was great, and you gobbled down a superhuman helping of ice cream, what's in your stomach, shark-in-a-cap?, and you went to bed, and we stayed up talking, and I smoked for the first time in months, and Mum didn't say anything, and then I just fell asleep, like I'd passed out, and as far as I know I didn't dream.

And what else? well, nothing, I got sicker and here I am, it was very soon after you left, do you remember how we said goodbye?, the two of us were in the garage, what a place for a ceremony, huh?, Mum was taking you to your grandparents, she sat in the car, she didn't get out, she preferred to leave us on our own, the drive would take three hours, and I asked you the time, and you looked at your watch proudly, and then I gave you a hug, a long hug, and I told you not to forget to fasten your seatbelt, that was it, that was all, all I was capable of saying was fasten your seatbelt, I'd even thought up an animal for you, a sea animal I guess, but I totally forgot, I'd imagined this scene so many times, I suppose this is what real goodbyes are like, right?, out of place, clumsy.

What I haven't forgotten, you see, is hugging you, I don't know what you felt, bah, I mean, whether you felt anything, I'm not sure I did right then either, what I know is what I feel now, when I look back, I remember so clearly the heat from your head, the smell of shampoo, the downy hair on the nape of your neck, that vertebra that sticks out more than the others, your pointy shoulders, and remembering these things, experiencing them all over again, is like untying myself, you understand?, and all of a sudden I stop envying healthy people, well, I'm lying, I still envy them, but I also pity them, do you know what the mother of a sick girl told me the other day?, that everyone had, what was it she said?, four dimensions, that we were born whole, and that— come in, yes, come in.

What was I going to?, oh yes, the four-dimensional thing, so this woman was telling me that we were already whole, that from the beginning our lives contained our birth and death, and that we only saw ourselves grow up or grow old because we perceived ourselves bit by bit, can you believe it?, but that actually the child and the old person exist simultaneously, or something like that, it sounded crazy to me, her daughter is dying and she tries to, to resign herself, you know?, to experience it as something natural, I'd understand much better, I don't know, if she went round kicking in monitors, pulling out cables, punching the doctors, I think it's, my forehead's a bit, I'm going to ask for a thermometer.

Your mum didn't want to leave, I had to insist, bah, to force her to, I've been thinking, you know?, about what I told you yesterday, about that poor woman, the thing that used to scare me most, was dying young, I was obsessed with reaching old age, I felt entitled, what a fool, right?, what's strange is to live the way I did when I was healthy, time is never long enough, it always, so to speak, falls short, they say the perfect way to die is in your sleep, without even noticing, I'm not so sure, I think I'd rather feel it, I want to live my death, it's all I have left, I don't want it taken away from me, when you reach my age, more or less, perhaps you'll start to feel protective, and you're not going to have a father to look after, there'll be no father to enable you to be that son, I'll be a lost opportunity, and so now, well, now comes the advice, I feel a bit ridiculous, the ideal thing would be for you to observe me half your life and think: all right, let's salvage this and this from the misguided man who is my father, and let the devil take the rest, too bad, we can't, we can't.

Enjoy life, do you hear?, it's hard work enjoying life, and have patience, not too much, and look after yourself as if you knew you won't always be young, even though you won't know it and that's okay, and have plenty of sex, son, do it for your sake and mine and even your mother's, lots of sex, and if you have children, have them late, and go to the beach in winter, in winter it's better, you'll see, my head hurts yet I feel good, it's hard to explain, and go travelling on your own once in a while, and try not to fall in love all the time, and care about your looks, do you hear me?, men who don't care about their looks are afraid of being queer, and if you are queer, be a man, in short, advice isn't much use, if you disagree with it you don't listen, and if you already agree you don't need it, never trust advice, son, travel agents advise you to go places they've never been, you'll love me more when you're old, I thought of my father the moment we got down from the truck, our true love for our parents is posthumous, forgive me for that, I'm already proud of the things you're going to do, I love the way you count the time on your fingers when you set the alarm clock, or do you think I don't see?, you do it secretly, under the covers, so I won't know you have difficulty working it out, I'm going to ask you a favour, whatever happens, whatever age you are, don't stop counting the time on your fingers, promise me, octopus.

It's getting dark there, in the window, your mum will be here soon, I'll go on tomorrow, I'm hungry, I'm sleepy, there's a new nurse who looks a lot like your mother when she was young, her name is Alicia, she's very kind, she's going to get me some pasta even though chicken's on the menu, Alicia is a good name for a girl, don't you think?

Lito

I open my eyes. The sun is in my face. Dad is taking the strips of plastic off the windows. I close my eyes again. I remember I was dreaming something really weird. We were going to the seaside. We who? Actually I think I was alone. I went down to the shore. And I started tearing strips off the water. Like it was an animal's skin. Below the sea the sun was buried. The more strips I tore, the more light I discovered. Then a fisherman appeared. Or somebody with a sort of tow truck. And he started taking away the bits of sea. Then Dad took the plastic off.

Good morning, meddlesome marmot, Dad says holding a piece of bread in one hand, ham or cheese? No tomato? I ask. There's none left, he answers. I lift my body off the mattress. I stretch. Ham and cheese, thanks, I say yawning. Hey, Dad, doesn't your back hurt? Mine, he answers, I don't have a back anymore.

We pass a sign that says: Valdemancha. This last day of our trip feels like the shortest. We've got the radio blaring. I follow the rhythm of the music with my legs. Dad hardly talks at all. I start counting every car we pass. Suddenly I have an idea. Dad, I say, can we go see the sea? He doesn't answer. I don't know if he's heard me. He doesn't even blink. But then all of a sudden he says: Yes we can. And he changes lane. And he takes the first exit.

We have lunch in Tres Torres. Dad tells me the town is called that because it used to have three castles. But now there's only one. So why don't they change the name, I ask. Meddlesome marmot, he answers. Dad spreads a map out on the table in the bar. He shows the detour we're making. He marks with a pencil the route we were going to take. And in red ink the one we're taking. He works out how long each bit should take. He writes a time next to each place. The red line zigzags along the coast. Dad seems excited now. This way, he says, we won't see the same things we saw on the way here, right? Yes, I say smiling. I love making plans with Dad.

Now we're on our way to the sea I concentrate really hard. I stare at Pedro's windscreen. The moment I see a cloud I look at the wipers and imagine them brushing it away. So far I'm doing okay because the sky is still blue. This road has tons of cars on it. We keep having to dodge them. Too bad Dad doesn't like video games. He'd beat my score if he wanted to. Or he'd equal it at least.

The smell is different. We don't even need to open the windows. The sea gets in anyway. I'm not sure how. But it does. I see it appear and disappear between bends. It's really shiny. Like millions of screens. It isn't blue. Or green. It's, I don't know. Sea colour.

At last! At last we arrive in Puerto del Este. I can see the harbour and sailboats. There are tons of people. And kids eating ice creams. I think Dad is checking out the girls. Mum doesn't look like that in a bikini. Some cyclists go by as well. Racing bikes are awesome. Especially if you have a helmet and stuff. I'm going to ask for one when I'm eleven. We're moving slowly. There's nowhere to park Pedro. We drive away from the harbour. I can see a campsite. And volleyball nets. We drive round and round. We stop at a piece of wasteland opposite the beach. As soon as Dad opens the doors, I jump out.

My skin is all cold and salty. My legs stick to the seat. Lito, Dad says, looking at me out of the corner of his eye. Dry your hair well. Or you'll catch a cold. But it's hot in here, I answer. Dad insists. I groan. Anyway, he's the one who's always getting colds. That's why he didn't go in the sea. I unstick my legs. Ouch! I reach out and grab the towel from the back seat. I rub my head. Good and hard. Until all of a sudden my heart jumps. My head! My cap! I search everywhere. I rummage through the swimming things. Through our bags. In the glove box. Under the seat. I can't believe it. I can't have lost the magician's cap. But how?, where?, what a dummy (What's wrong, son? Dad says), I'm the biggest dummy on the planet, I'll never find another one like it, there are zillions of baseball caps, of course, but this one, this exact one (Do you need something, son? Dad asks) is impossible to buy, maybe I lost it on the beach?, wasn't I wearing it in the truck?, then it has to be here (Put your seatbelt back on, Dad says, right now, Lito, okay, thank you), or was I stupid enough to wear it in the sea?, it could be, because I ran straight in, or maybe it fell off while I was running?, I can't believe it, I hate myself, I hate myself, and on top of that, what a sissy (Lito, what's wrong? Dad says slowing down, come on, no, don't cry), it isn't just the cap, I'm also crying because there's no way, no way Dad can understand how special that cap was (Hey, son, come here, he says reaching out and putting his arm around me), I cling to him, I hide my face in his shirt (I'm so sorry, he says stroking me, so sorry), and suddenly Dad seems like he's going to start crying about my cap too.

I sit up. I wipe my nose. And I tell him about it. Even though

I'm ashamed. Dad agrees it must have blown away on the beach. He tries to cheer me up by playing the fool. Maybe it really was a magic cap, he says, and it flew off by itself. I get annoyed. I laugh a bit. I cry some more. And I calm down. Dad accelerates again. I slide my hand toward his head. I touch his neck. His ears. His shaved head. Suddenly I feel like having the same haircut as him. Dad, I say, how about if I shave my head this summer? He pulls his head away. We'll think about it, he answers, we'll think about it.

We have a snack in a café full of mirrors. It has a super long bar. It looks even longer in the mirrors. I'm not sure where we are. There are trucks like ours opposite the entrance. So I guess we're back on our road again. I order a glass of hot milk, jam on toast, and a chocolate croissant. Dad orders a black coffee. A few days ago I was getting a bit fed up with travelling. Sometimes I thought about going home. Seeing Mum. Having my toys again. Now I'm sad the trip is almost over. Dad gets up to make a call. I watch him move along the mirrors. He signals to me to stay here. I hope he doesn't take long. It's so boring waiting for him. I finish my snack. I look round. Everyone else seems to be doing something. Except me. There's a shop at the far end selling cheese, newspapers, CDs, and other stuff. I'd like to go and see it. I order another glass of milk. Suddenly Dad is in the shop. Like he'd appeared through one of the mirrors. After a while he comes back. He pays. And he asks me to go.

I stare at the lines on the road trying not to blink. They look like they're moving. I imagine somebody's firing rays at us. A tank filled with avenger soldiers. A racing car with a laser gun. I don't say these things to Dad anymore. He's always telling me about the victims of war and stuff like that. Dad's a real bore that way now. Before it was Mum who gave me lectures about peace. And Dad would say: It's okay, Elena, best let him get it out of his system. But now Dad gives me Mum's lectures. (Lito.) And she gets less worried. (Lito.) She's got more used to it. (Lito, my love.) Except about food. (Son, I'm talking to you.) Maybe Dad's this way because we're travelling. We'll see at home. (Hey! Are you listening to me?)

Yes, yes, I answer. Dad smiles. Pass my shades, will you? he says. No, the other ones, yes those, thanks. I give him his shades. He is still looking at me. Didn't you notice anything? he asks. Where? I say. In the glove box, son, in the glove box, he answers. There's loads of stuff in there. Papers. Files. Cables. Tools. CDs. Open it again, says Dad. Oof. I open it again. And among all the stuff I see a small package. A small package wrapped in gift paper. I don't wait for Dad to say anything else. I start tearing off the wrapping paper. I nearly break the box. And at last I manage to open it. And I see it, I see it, I see it. And I take it out of the box and hold it up and look at it closely and put it on. I can't believe I'm wearing a Lewis Valentino. A submersible. With a light. And the date. And everything. Then I remember to hug Dad.

I recognize these rocks. The dry ground. Tucumancha. The edges of the highway are very close. Dad asks what time it is. Aha! I turn my wrist slowly. I stare at the hands of my watch. Just to be sure I press the little knob for the light. And I tell him the exact time. With minutes and seconds. Dad says: It's late. And he accelerates. To tell the truth, I'm in no hurry.

There are trees again at the sides. And fields. And animals. The highway is wider. Pedro is going super fast. Dad's phone beeps. He says: Tell her we're almost there. And that I'll call her in a bit.

I read:

Angel how many more miles? I (Dad accelerates some more and turns on the headlights) can't wait to see you.

How's Daddy? I've cooked (we drive fast round the bends, my body flops to one side) a yummy homecoming meal! I (the grass changes colour, the faster we go the more yellow, or brown it is) love you to pieces (I open the window so I can see better, I stick my head out and Dad closes it).

I type:

```
d sz we r v nr wl cl u sn xx
```

We pass Pampatoro. It starts getting dark. There's still a tiny bit of sun. Like it has steam in it. I can see shadows of trees. We pass other headlights. The animals almost don't have heads.

Suddenly I see a raindrop on the window. And another. And another. A line of them. Several lines. A stream of raindrops. It's weird. Really weird. I was super happy. I concentrate on the windscreen wipers. I imagine they're sweeping the sky. Hitting the clouds like tennis balls. And the clouds are falling on the other side of the fields. Miles away. The windscreen wipers start to move. Small puddles form on the window then break up. I don't believe this. I try to think about funny things. I remember jokes. I force myself to smile until my cheeks ache. I sing. I whistle. I try to imagine a round moon. Like a big clean plate. The sky grows dark. The clouds have spots all over them. Pedro's roof makes more noise. The windscreen is flooded. The wipers are moving faster and faster. I don't believe this. I ask Dad why it's raining so much. He touches my fringe. The window is blurred.

Suddenly I get it. *Peter–bilt!*

Elena

A forest on my bookshelves and a desert in my house. Yet, no matter how far I venture into the forest, I always come across the same desert. As though all the books in the world, whatever they are about, spoke to me of death.

Stories, stories, stories. Escapes, detours, shortcuts.

How Mario would have loved this collection of letters between Chekhov and the actress Olga Knipper, consorts at a distance. He always travelling, she always in the theatre. Both speaking of future re-encounters. Until their correspondence is interrupted. And toward the end, suddenly, like an improvisation amid an empty stage, she starts to write to her deceased husband. "So, as I write," she says to herself, she says to him, "I feel you are awaiting my letter."

If death interrupts all dialogues, it is only natural to write posthumous letters. Letters to the one who isn't there. Because he isn't. So that he is. Maybe this is what all writing is.

Do you agree? I have such a lot to tell you. And even a lot to ask you.

Let's say you said yes.

Dear Mario, I have put a photo of you in the living room. I write *living room*, and realize for how long you haven't lived with us while we had meals, relaxed, watched TV. Companionship isn't about experiencing great moments together. True companionship is the other stuff. Sharing a sincere doing nothing.

I put you on one of the highest shelves, near the window, so that you can breathe or amuse yourself a little. Until recently I felt incapable of looking at photos of you. It was like moving my hand toward a sharp object. You gazed into my eyes so trustingly, so shamelessly alive. Those photos triggered in me a feeling of unreality in the opposite direction: what was impossible, dream-like, was outside the portrait. Not you on that side, grinning. Us here, now. This half a house.

Before, when we used to look at photos of me in a bikini back when we were dating, so skinny, with flowing hair, firm breasts, I felt insulted. As though someone had touched my arse and, when I turned round, there wasn't anyone there. These days I need to go back to our early pictures, to spy on us in our youth. Seeing us cheerful, not suspecting the future, I have the impression I am regaining a certainty. That the past wasn't my invention. That we were there, somewhere in time.

Looking at you again when you were beautiful, I wonder whether I am celebrating or denying you. Whether I am recalling you as you actually were or forgetting you when you were sick. Reflecting about it today (if pain can be reflected about and doesn't disperse like a gas under the pressure of reason), the biggest injustice about your illness was the feeling that this man was no longer you, that you were gone. But you weren't: he, this, was my man. Your worn-out body. The last of you.

When I placed you among the books, Lito came over, he stood staring at the photo and said nothing. After a while he went into his room and came out with a ball.

I remember, do you remember?, do the departed retain something, somehow?, when we ran into each other at university. You were strolling with your hands in your jean pockets, greeting the girls as you went by, as though you were just visiting. You looked at us with the expression of a marauding prole. I dethrone princesses, you seemed to be saying to us. You sauntered among the desks with the air of knowing far more urgent things than Latin. That was what irritated me. That was what seduced me. Despite all your boasting to the contrary, you actually liked studying. What you disliked was being a student. "I don't mind having to read all this stuff," you would say to me. "But having to prove it to some moron in a suit," you protested, you swaggered, "is insulting." What a liar, how handsome I thought you were.

Meanwhile, there I was attending lectures from Monday to Friday. Scrupulously taking notes. Studying on Saturdays (what a dummy!). Graduating with honours. Passing my exams early. Believing that way I would secure some certainty from among the many daunting possibilities. We used to say my vocation was clearer than yours. That wasn't the whole truth. A vocation is a never-ending mission. In other words, a refined way of avoiding the unknown. You weren't afraid of the unknown. Perhaps that's why you died first.

And I remember how planning trips for others bored you, how you dreamt of quitting the travel agency, and your brother insisted you should give Pedro a try. What a notion. I gradually got used to that name. To the point where whenever I saw a truck I thought of Pedro. I never told you this. The way you never told me that, one fine day, you stopped paying the car insurance. I found out last week, when I tried to buy a cheaper insurance. Where did that money go? What happened to the fixed-term deposit? It no longer matters. A secret for a secret.

"One night, while he was waiting for them to kill him at any moment," I catch my breath in a novel by Irène Némirovsky, "he had seen the house in her dream, as now, through the window," some nights, facing our bedroom window, as my book slips from my hands, I see you smoking on the balcony, crinkling up your eyes at the same time as me, and everything grows dark, and you are like an ember flaring up and going out, "he had awoken with a start," the book falls to the floor, I open my eyes suddenly, I look out at the balcony, there is nobody, "and thought: Only before death can one remember in this way."

Today, when I checked my bank balance, I discovered I had more money than yesterday. I stood holding the slip of paper and calculating, adding up days, subtracting expenditures, motionless before the cash machine. Today wasn't payday. No one owed me money.

At home I examined my account over the last few months. I made a printout: a plummeting balance and then a sudden peak. I imagined a plane diving into the sea, and the pilot waking up with a start.

The transfer had no reference. The entry was blank. I emailed my bank to find out which account it came from. For an instant, my heart stopped: the surname was yours.

The first name was Juanjo's.

❖ ❖ ❖

When I met you, you were in the habit of travelling every summer. You would make decisions on the spur of the moment. You came and went. You already lived as if you were in a travel agency. You were always more adventurous than I. But every epic has its cook. Because to go on an adventure, and this problem dates back to Homer, every hero needs someone to admire them, to wait for them.

And the one who stayed behind studying, while you reflected about the freedom of the wanderer, was this idiot here.

This is me: in order to forgive, I need to regret something even worse.

❖ ❖ ❖

I just survived a movie by Susanne Bier, distressing, like all Scandinavian movies. In it a kid says:

"Grown-ups look like kids when they're dead. My mother looked like a kid. Like she'd never grown up. Like she'd never been a mother."

In an attempt to explain the inexplicable, the doctor says:

"There's a curtain between the living and the dead. Sometimes this curtain goes up. For example, when you lose a loved one. Then, for an instant, you see death very clearly. Afterward the curtain comes down again. You carry on living. And it passes."

The kid simply replies:

"Are you sure?"

❖ ❖ ❖

A surprise: my sister is here. Can you believe it?

In fact, she told me last week she had booked a flight. But since, as you know, she usually changes her plans at the last minute, I wasn't going to take her arrival as a given until I saw her at the airport. It's been a while since we touched each other. You can't see the grey hairs, wrinkles, thickening waist, and heavy hips so well on the screen. I thought she had lost her looks. I wonder how I must seem to her, now I am no longer the younger sister but the widow.

Since your illness, it no longer surprises me to hear about other people's misfortunes. I respond as if they had already told me. What shocks me is the way the lives of others seem to carry on as before. I felt this when I embraced my sister, and, after so long, she smiled uneasily and told me, yes, things were fine, as always.

Once we were in the car, she asked about Lito. She calls him *my nephew* and she barely knows him. Before she arrived, I thought I'd show our son some photos of his aunt. And I realized he couldn't really point her out. As soon as she looked younger or wore her hair differently, he no longer recognized her. At first, I was exasperated with him. I raised my voice, I complained he never paid attention, I wouldn't let him have chocolate. Then I blamed myself for restricting relations with the family, for having come between Lito and your brothers. Then I took offence at my sister for not calling enough, hardly ever writing, not visiting us more: all those things that, in theory, had never bothered me. In the end I thought I understood where my anger came from. If my son had trouble recognizing his aunt, that meant before long he would start being unsure about your face.

Sisterhood is perplexing. It can transport us, in a flash, from the most sinister aloofness to a complete identification, or vice versa. As we drove together in the car, changing topics, the way one changes channels in search of an interesting programme, something gave way inside me. The defensive muscle that reacts whenever we meet. We agreed a couple of times, laughed a bit. Then I took my eyes off the road and glanced at her again, without suspicion. I caught myself thinking she had actually aged well. I am the one who, terrified, sees myself in her, as if my older sister were the chronicle of my next decade.

Since she landed, she has been trying to show a degree of protectiveness toward me. Perhaps she still feels guilty for not having come when you died. There is no reason she should: I myself insisted she wasn't going to arrive in time for the wake. I sense she wants to broach the subject, but I don't give her a chance. I know what each of us would say. I have listened to that conversation, over and over, talking to myself. Arguing with my sister is like shouting at a concave mirror. I don't recognize the person before me, yet she seems disturbingly similar.

"I was a married woman," recalls the character in a novel by César Aira. "We always hesitate," I underline, "before erasing the evidence of something that happened," what happened is the only thing we have now, and it is destined to be lost. "Almost everything that happens scarcely leaves traces in our memory," memory is a delicate skin, skin has a short memory, "and memory isn't trustworthy, isn't even credible." I deleted all your e-mails, your text messages, your work files. I noticed no relief.

"It was my hands versus my head," to do in order not to think, not to think about what to do. "The voluptuousness I felt when penetrating my mental labyrinths made me realize it was dangerous ground," every labyrinth is dangerously intimate, "but this feeling only increased my pleasure, and my guilt, which were one and the same thing," to the point where this voluptuousness no longer depended on what I did with Ezequiel. It was in me, like a medical after-effect.

I needed someone to hear it. I have just told my sister what you already know, what you never knew. Or did you?

We were both in the bedroom. Braiding each other's hair the way we did as kids. The way we did during our summers at the beach house. One leaning her head against the other's stomach, letting her hair be caressed. And then we would change places. We spoke in those hushed tones that enable you to say the first thing that comes into your head. This is how I confided to her about Ezequiel. My sister was braiding my hair. I noticed her stomach tense. She scarcely drew breath while I spoke. She exhaled slowly, like when you do prenatal exercises. Predictably, she responded with shock. Something which, in her own way, she also needed to do. My sister has no problem understanding immoral acts, so long as it remains clear from the outset that she would never commit them herself.

I must admit she didn't try to judge me before I finished telling the whole story. Next, she declared herself "physically incapable" (her exact words, my darling) of having a lover. And least of all, she continued, modulating her voice with exemplariness, in a situation like the one you and I had been through. "A situation," she said. I wanted to tear her hair out. I replied that it was quite the opposite. That, physically speaking, the most natural thing was to have a lover. And most of all, I spelt it out, straightening up, in desperate situations.

This was as far as my arguments went. After that, what came out was my own unmistakeable rubbish. We argued for a while.

Until it occurred to me to tell her: You have enough trouble with your own husband, who unfortunately is alive and kicking.

My sister left the bedroom without uttering a word. I heard her moving stuff around. And the door go at the end of the hallway. A few minutes later I received a text message (typical of her: polite, dignified, insufferable) informing me she was going to visit our parents.

Wretchedly I replied:

```
I'm sure you'll be on your best behaviour with
them.
```

"Suffering that is too apparent doesn't inspire pity," I verify in an essay by Philippe Ariès, "but rather revulsion." We tolerate, are even pleased, that others suffer, but not when it splashes us, this is already "a sign of mental disorder or rudeness." "Within the family circle we are still wary, for fear of upsetting the children," although if we knew how to raise kids properly, on the contrary, they would be upset by the lack of obvious suffering at the loss of a loved one. "We only have the right to cry," we only grant ourselves this right, "if no one either sees or hears us," confined in our room, doubly confined, "solitary shameful grieving is the only option, like masturbation," besides shame, is there some pleasure, there? "The comparison is made by Gorer," I don't know who he is, but I want a date with him.

I search for Gorer, I find him, he wanted to be a writer, he failed (welcome to the club, Geoffrey), he became an anthropologist, he researched de Sade (a sadist, then) and ended up studying sex in marriage (precisely, a sadist). I find the quote "At present, death and mourning are treated with much the same prudery as sexual impulses were a century ago," is prudishness therefore suffering in secret, masturbating with mourning? "So that it need be given no public expression," so that it doesn't soil the clothes of others, "and indulged, if at all, in private . . . furtively," I've never been introduced to a Geoffrey.

My love, your crazy widow here.

Shall we get to the point?

Sometimes, at night, alone in our bedroom, I am tempted to contact Ezequiel. I take pleasure in imagining that I have. And I know I would do again all the things I did.

If I don't call him it is more out of pride than remorse. After all, I myself forbade him to see me again. How could he have obeyed me so instantly?

Men's obsession with being consistent horrifies me.

A message from my sister:

    Mum and Dad have sold the beach house. I assume
    you knew. Wish you'd told me. Love from all 3.

No, I didn't know.
They always seemed to be fine there.

And wouldn't it have been better to think about it a little longer? I insisted, we had so many good summers at that house. The way things stood, my love, there wasn't much time for thought, my mother explained, the bills were very high, it needed work, we could no longer even afford the maintenance. Really? I said, why didn't you tell me? Because you never asked, my mother replied calmly.

Lito just came home from school with a split lip. He is happy. He says he is learning to command respect.

I was horrified to see him with blood on his mouth. But I assumed if I showed my dismay, he would shut me out. I know there are macho issues that only macho men can understand, and all that bullshit philosophy. So I forced myself to behave naturally. I swear to you I smiled, I smiled when confronted by our wounded son!, provided he told me what had happened.

When he saw I was on his side, Lito gave me a blow-by-blow account of how the fight came about. The precise insults exchanged. Whereabouts in the playground the fight had taken place. Exactly how he had hit the other boy. His story sounded like a sports commentary. I breathed deeply in order not to feel sick. While treating his lip, as if in passing, I asked who he had defended himself against so successfully.

When he pronounced the boy's name I had to stop myself from bursting into tears. I knew the kid. He is timid. A squirt. One of the smallest boys in his class. I once spoke to his mother, who lives in constant fear of him getting hurt. The poor kid has trouble scraping through physical education. This was the boy Lito had hit until it made him feel better.

So explain to me. You. The father. The man. How the hell does one deal with this sort of thing? What stories did your son bring home to you from school? How did you respond? Did you preach to him about pacifism? Did you lie to him? Did you teach him how to throw a punch? Did you tell him how much you liked fighting when you were a kid? How come you just stay there, dead?

I have started two books by Christian Bobin. I alternate, like headphones playing different music for each ear. I read in stereo.

I am depressed as I underline in the first book:

"The event is what is alive, and what is alive does not protect itself from loss." So, the true event is loss?

I laugh as I underline in the second book:

"Young mothers have affairs with the invisible. And, because they have affairs with the invisible, young mothers end up becoming invisible. Men are unaware that such things happen. This may even be man's function: not to see the invisible." So, the invisible man is the true man?

Let's be honest. All honesty is a little posthumous. To you, your son's day-to-day life was like a favourite TV series. You followed it with interest, but because you always missed half the episodes, you couldn't understand the whole plot. But you had the father you had. And that was excuse enough for you to emerge unscathed.

I remember once, I was with your mother in the kitchen. We were chopping vegetables to make soup. Your mother was incredible with a knife: I've never seen transparent slices like those since. You were smoking in the living room with your father and brothers. All of a sudden the lights went out. Your mother lit a candle, and we went out into the hallway. That narrow hallway in your parents' house. She opened the fuse box, held the candle up, and pointed to the fuse that had just blown. She quickly closed it, without touching anything. And we went back into the kitchen. From there, we heard your father's booming voice, his footsteps with yours, the sound of the fuse box opening. Sometimes, your mother whispered to me in the candlelight, you have to let them believe they are the ones with the solution.

I had the phone in my hand, lying on the bed, sending my messages, I saw his name in my contact list and, suddenly, without thinking, I pressed Ezequiel's number.

His voicemail came on. I hung up.

He didn't even return the call.

When I see a couple kissing, believing they love one another, believing they will endure, whispering into each other's ear in the name of an instinct to which they give lofty names, when I see them caressing one another with that embarrassing avidness, that expectation of discovering something crucial in the other's skin, when I see their mouths becoming entangled, the exchange of tongues, their freshly showered hair, their unruly hands, fabric rubbing and lifting up like the most sordid of curtains, the anxious tic of knees bouncing like springs, cheap beds in one-night hotels they will later remember as palaces, when I see two fools expressing their desire with impunity in broad daylight, as though I weren't watching them, it's not merely envy I feel. I also pity them. I pity their rotten future. And I get up and ask for the bill and I smile at them askance, as though I had returned from a war which the two of them have no idea is about to commence.

I confess to you that I have sometimes felt jealous. Not of other women you perhaps knew. Jealous of our son. I know it is ugly. I am ugly.

When Lito talks about you, when he half-remembers, half-invents you, I realize he is an orphan with two fathers. The father he had, made of flesh and doubts. And this other phantom father who watches over his adventures, and, however foolish they are, applauds them. Apparently, this second version of you understands our son better than anyone. The less he knows you, the more he admires you.

Occasionally, a touch of fear underlying his curiosity, Lito asks me about the accident, because we always refer to it as *The Accident*, like the name of a movie by someone we don't know, and when our son says *The Accident*, I am seduced into believing this is what dying is, a misfortune that befell you and will never affect us, that can never affect him, he is my son, he is immortal.

We are brought up being told that sons maintain an umbilical tie with their mothers. I want to earn my son's admiration, not to take it for granted because I gave birth to him. That's the difference between a mother and a mammal. Love of the father is only attained over time. It is won. That is what I envy about you. Just imagine how it is now that, on top of everything else, you are a Phantom Dad.

You find it funny, my love? Go to hell.

Do you need money? my sister asked in that responsible tone my Dad admires so much. No, I pretended, why do you ask? No reason, she replied, how much do you need? When I said the amount I felt odd, grateful, younger.

In his autobiography, Richard Gwyn describes how a liver transplant saved his life. The liver Roberto Bolaño was waiting for, the one his specialist was unable to find for Bolaño while he dedicated his final lecture to him, the liver Gwyn restores to Bolaño.

"The thought occurs to me that I spent ten years studying and writing about the subjectivity of the patient, that I have a PhD in the narrative construction of illness experience, have published in learned journals and even written a couple of books on the subject," I know the feeling: being sick from sickness. "None of this can help me now. I am in a post-discursive zone. I have reached The End of Theory," an end which, of course, doesn't cure us of anything either, except perhaps of the hope of ever finding The Remedy, The Idea, The Understanding of the Phenomenon, culturally contagious diseases.

Gwyn speaks of two kingdoms which believe they are opposed, that of sickness and that of health. He has lived in both, like you, and he is no longer sure which is his. "It is as if I hold two passports from countries that are mutually suspicious of each other." We subjects of the kingdom of the healthy mistrust our future kingdom. We take careful note of it. We pretend to accept it by objectifying it. We examine it in search of some diplomatic passport that will spare us the sordid formalities.

Dear, daily Mario. Today, without knowing why, I enjoyed myself quite a lot. Perhaps because nothing out of the ordinary happened.

The next step, and this is also going to hurt, will be to let joy in. If it comes. If I recognize it. I can already sense the next blow: not of loss, but of guilt because of fresh gains. Like today, for instance. Like this shameless sunlight pouring through our bedroom window, akin to a child smashing vases.

It scares me sometimes when occasionally, for a moment, I forget you. Then I hasten to write. You can't complain. Even forgetting you reminds me of you.

I thought (beloved platitude) that the worst thing about losing you would be not having you. But it isn't; you are still there, I think of you while I talk to myself. I don't want to get too esoteric, so let's just say you have become part of my organism. Now that I am growing accustomed to being alone (or at most, on a Saturday, being with I don't know who), the worst thing is accepting that I am not in you. I am no longer part of you. Looked at in this way, I have also died.

But will you look at that sun, what a rascal.

I remember our conversations at the hospital. Not so much because of what we said to each other (there were no revelations, at least no spoken revelations), but because of the absurd miracle of being able to talk to someone who was dying, who was already leaving and who went on talking. I remember one conversation in particular. You were lying down with your eyes open. I was sitting by your bed. From time to time we stroked one another. Chastely, as once before. It was a mild afternoon. You seemed

calm. You were gazing out of the window. Are you ready? I asked.
And I squeezed your hand. Are you? you asked me. I don't remember what my reply was.

I have just been to Ezequiel's office. I didn't call. I didn't make
an appointment. I simply turned up, sat in the waiting room, and
stared at that door we know so well.

I exchanged a few words with the patients sitting next to me.
They all assumed I was there for the same reasons as them. Every
so often, they stood up, gave me a token smile, and went into the
examination room. Someone else would immediately arrive to
take their place.

I saw people our age, adolescents, old people, children. I saw
fathers, grandfathers, friends, aunts. I saw men and women,
some better dressed than others. They all looked ugly to me.
They were all beautiful.

Have you been waiting long? a lady on her own enquired sym-
pathetically. Quite a while, I replied, and you? All afternoon, she
said, I prefer to get here early, it puts my mind at ease.

Suddenly Ezequiel's voice filtered through the door, Dr. Escalante's tone. It grew louder. It vibrated. It reached the doorway.
It mingled with two other fainter voices. Then Ezequiel's groomed
head appeared, his whole body emerged, dressed in white. He was
with an elderly couple, the man very serious, the woman trying to
smile. Ezequiel stood between the two of them. He had a hand
on each of their shoulders. As they stepped through the doorway,
the three instantly dropped their voices. Their six feet stopped
on the threshold of the waiting room. I focused on Ezequiel's
face. On his rippling eyebrows. On his way of speaking, almost

without opening his lips. He said goodbye to the couple. I quickly lowered my head. I don't think he saw me.

When the door closed once more, I stood up and left behind the elderly couple. They were taking small steps. I copied their rhythm. I walked with them. I followed them for a while, gazing at their backs.

A Note on Translations

There follows a list of the works cited by Elena in this novel. The translation of passages originally published in languages other than English was done by Nick Caistor and Lorenza Garcia. If writing allows us to talk to ourselves, reading and translating are very much like having a conversation.

A.N.

Aira, César. *Yo era una mujer casada.* Santiago de Chile. Cuneta, 2010.

Ariès, Philippe. "La mort interdite." In *Essais sur l'histoire de la mort en Occident du Moyen Âge à nos jours.* Paris: Seuil, 1975.

Atwood, Margaret. "Let Us Now Praise Stupid Women." In *Good Bones.* Toronto: Coach House Press, 1992.

Banville, John. *The Sea.* London: Picador, 2005.

Bobin, Christian. *Autoportrait au radiateur.* Paris: Gallimard, 1997.

———. *La part manquante.* Paris: Gallimard, 1989.

Bolaño, Roberto. "Literatura + enfermedad = enfermedad." In *El gaucho insufrible.* Barcelona: Anagrama, 2003.

Chekhov, Anton, and Olga Knipper. Letter from Olga, August 19, 1904. In *Correspondencia 1899–1904.* Edited and translated from the Russian into Spanish by Paul Viejo. Madrid: Páginas de Espuma, 2008.

Ford, Richard. *The Sportswriter.* New York: Vintage, 1986.

Garner, Helen. *The Spare Room.* Melbourne: Text Publishing, 2008.

Gorer, Geoffrey. *Death, Grief, and Mourning in Contemporary Britain.* London: Cresset Press, 1965.

Gracia Armendáriz, Juan. *Diario del hombre pálido*. Madrid: Demipage, 2010.

Gwyn, Richard. *The Vagabond's Breakfast*. Aberystwyth (U.K.): Alcemi, 2011.

Levrero, Mario. *La novela luminosa*. Montevideo: Alfaguara, 2005.

Marías, Javier. *Los enamoramientos*. Madrid: Alfaguara, 2011.

Matute, Ana María. *Los niños tontos*. Barcelona: Destino, 1956.

Moore, Lorrie. "People Like That Are the Only People Here: Canonical Babbling in Peed Onk." In *Birds of America*. New York: Alfred A. Knopf, 1998.

Navarro, Justo. *La casa del padre*. Barcelona: Anagrama, 1994.

Némirovsky, Irène. *Les Mouches d'automne*. Paris: Grasset, 1931.

O'Connor, Flannery. "The Enduring Chill." In *Everything That Rises Must Converge*. New York: Farrar, Straus and Giroux, 1965.

Ōe, Kenzaburō. *A Personal Matter*. New York: Grove Press, 1969; *Una cuestión personal*. Barcelona: Anagrama, 1989.

Ozick, Cynthia. "Puttermesser: Her Work History, Her Ancestry, Her Afterlife." In *The Puttermesser Papers*. New York: Alfred A. Knopf, 1997.

Uhart, Hebe. "¿Cómo vuelvo?" In *Del cielo a casa*. Buenos Aires: Adriana Hidalgo editora, 2003.

Woolf, Virginia. *On Being Ill*. London: Hogarth Press, 1930.